Newfoundland Stories

Newfoundland Stories

THE LOSS OF THE WATERWITCH
and other tales

ELDON DRODGE

dedicated

to my four grandsons,

Daniel

Zachary

Benjamin

Jack

Library and Archives Canada Cataloguing in Publication

Drodge, Eldon, 1942-
Newfoundland stories : the loss of the waterwitch and other tales / Eldon Drodge.
ISBN 978-1-55081-331-9
I. Title
PS8557.R62N48 2010   C818'.6   C2010-905852-6

BREAKWATER BOOKS
WWW.BREAKWATERBOOKS.COM

We acknowledge the support of the Canada Council for the Arts which last year invested $1.3 million in the arts in Newfoundland. We acknowledge the Government of Canada through the Canada Book Fund and the Government of Newfoundland and Labrador through the Department of Tourism, Culture and Recreation for our publishing activities.

PRINTED IN CANADA.

Canada Council   Conseil des Arts
for the Arts   du Canada

Newfoundland
Labrador

Mixed Sources
Product group from well-managed forests, and other controlled sources
www.fsc.org Cert no. SW-COC-002358
© 1996 Forest Stewardship Council
FSC

contents

The Loss of the *Waterwitch* 9

The Hanging of Eleanor Power 20

Two Brothers 28

Pius Carroll Goes Swiling 38

Home from the War 47

The Light in the Garden 58

On Gander Lake 64

The Skraeling 72

The Drunk 90

The Fugitive 96

Maggie's Lament 101

Indian Killers 109

The New Road 126

What Happened at Devil's Cove? 138

Some of these stories are based on actual events and real characters.
The others are purely from the imagination.
All embody the essence of Newfoundland, past and present.

THE LOSS OF
THE WATERWITCH

amuel Spracklin, captain and owner of the *Waterwitch*, was worried. Having departed from St. John's in the early evening, his schooner, with twenty-five passengers and crew on board, was beating into the teeth of a northwesterly gale in late November 1875, en route to her home port of Cupids in Conception Bay. After more than three hours of hard sailing under full canvas, the vessel was still only abreast of Flatrock, a mere fifteen miles out of St. John's with another thirty-five miles to go, and the storm was intensifying. The other twenty-four people she was carrying, including Spracklin's son, Samuel, Jr., were equally apprehensive. Darkness and driving snow had diminished visibility to almost zero and the *Waterwitch* was taking on water each time her gunnels were raked and pulled under by the oncoming waves.

The weather had been a bit on the rough side when they left, but Spracklin had been undeterred and had sailed without a moment's hesitation. He had often taken his sturdy vessel out in weather as bad or worse without any problems. His ship's load included the winter provisions – food, clothing, and other necessities they would need to sustain them through the coming winter months – and he was anxious to get home to Cupids with his cargo. This would be his last voyage for the year. Within the next couple of weeks the *Waterwitch* would be berthed in Cupids for the winter and would remain tied up there until the following spring.

He had reckoned on making Cape St. Francis inside of three or four hours, and would then be able to take his vessel home comfortably in the lee shore of Conception Bay. At the time of his departure, he could not have anticipated the serious deterioration in the weather or the sudden shifting of the wind from the northeast to northwesterly. He briefly considered turning around and heading back to St. John's with the wind on their stern, but it was only a few more miles to the Cape, after which they should be okay, so he opted to continue on. With darkness and swirling snow limiting his vision and with no way of taking a reading to confirm his exact location, he was relying totally on his compass, his knowledge of winds and tides, and his long years of experience on the sea. Above all else, he knew that he dare not venture too close to the treacherous coastline in this area or he would run the risk of his schooner being dashed to pieces on the rocks.

Another hour of torturous progress saw them just off Pouch Cove, the last settlement before Cape St. Francis. The *Waterwitch* was by then being battered mercilessly, and the crew worked feverishly to keep her bow to the wind and to pump out the water that rushed in every time the schooner plummeted into the cavernous troughs that separated the towering waves. Most of the crew members were seasoned seamen, but few of them had ever experienced sea conditions as bad as this before. For despite Spracklin's calculations, the wind and the tides had carried the vessel much closer to the rocky shore than anyone on board realized, and when this fatal mistake was discovered it was too late to do anything about it. The *Waterwitch* was minutes away from crashing onto the rocks, and Spracklin and his crew, knowing their vessel was doomed, frantically tried to lower canvas as they braced themselves for the impact.

The crash, when it came, was horrendous. Some on board, including the four women, were either thrown from the vessel and dashed against the rocks or cast into the churning water. Some were killed outright in the crash. Of the twenty-five who had started the voyage, only thirteen, including Spracklin and his son, were left alive, and barring divine intervention, they too would soon follow their unfortunate shipmates.

The *Waterwitch* was wedged between two large rocks at the base of a towering cliff and, with any luck, might conceivably remain intact there for a while. Spracklin knew, however, the ship would eventually be battered to pieces by the pounding sea. He concluded that their only chance for survival rested on one of them scaling the cliff, finding help, and getting back before the vessel was destroyed.

He decided that he would be the one to try to climb the cliff. He selected one other seaman from his remaining crew to accompany him, Richard Ford,[1] a man whom he knew from personal experience to be strong and daring, and one with whom he could place his complete trust. Their first major hurdle was to make it from the vessel onto the rocks and then to the cliff. The courageous manoeuvre required agility and precise timing, and both men, after a number of false starts, soon found themselves standing on a narrow ledge at the base of the cliff. Their ascent could not be delayed, for with every passing second they were exposed to the risk of being sucked into the sea by the pounding surf that drove at them and saturated their clothes.

The ledge on which they stood zigzagged steeply upward for about a hundred feet before terminating into the face of the cliff, and the two men were able to cover that valuable ground in short order. Then their real difficulties began. From there to the top there was nothing but slippery, precipitous granite. Searching for finger and foot holds, Spracklin and Ford began a journey more dangerous that any other they would ever undertake in their lifetimes: the remaining four hundred feet to the top. By virtue of great physical strength and enormous willpower, they inched their way upward. Twenty minutes later, they could no longer hear the shouts of the stranded men over the blasting of the wind.

---

[1] It is not known for certain that Richard Ford was actually the man chosen to scale the cliff with Captain Spracklin.

They pressed their bodies tightly into the face of the cliff to keep from falling backward, as their numbed fingers guided their way in the darkness. In places, the cliff face was impossible to surmount, and the duo had to retreat or move laterally to try another approach. Frequent rests were needed to conserve their strength. Spracklin doubted that any of the others left on the schooner would have been capable of scaling this part of the cliff. Finally, sensing that they must be near the top, the two men marshalled the last of their waning energy for the final push to the summit. To their great relief, they were able to grasp the branches of the windswept spruce trees that overhung the edge of the cliff and pull themselves over the top. It had taken them almost half an hour to scale a height of five hundred feet.

Their job, however, was not yet done. They now had to find their way to a community and try to organize a party of rescuers. This presented Spracklin with another dilemma, for he didn't know which way to go. He had already made a fatal error in allowing the *Waterwitch* to drift so close to the shore. He knew that if he guessed incorrectly now the people he had left behind would surely be doomed. The responsibility weighed heavily on his mind. He believed that his vessel had come ashore somewhere in the vicinity of Pouch Cove, but he wasn't certain this was actually the case. If they had passed Pouch Cove before crashing and he went north, there was nothing but Cape Francis. If, on the other hand, they hadn't quite reached Pouch Cove, and he went south, they would have to follow the cliffs all the way back to Shoe Cove, a distance of several miles. Both of these scenarios would be disastrous. His only chance of success rested on them getting to Pouch Cove.

Realizing that every minute was crucial, the captain wracked his mind. His gut told him south. After a quick exchange with Ford, they decided that this was the way they would go. This time his decision would prove correct.

The *Waterwitch* had been driven ashore about a mile from the community of Pouch Cove, a distance which can be comfortably covered in twenty minutes or less in normal conditions. Though in the obscuring storm, it took Spracklin and Ford almost twice that long to reach the most northerly house in the community. Fortunately, even though it was now well past midnight, a light still shone in its window.

Eli Langmead was startled by unruly pounding on his door. He hesitated briefly before answering, fearful of the mischief makers that might be afoot at this late hour. When he did open the door, he was shocked by the two storm-battered men who stood there. He saw immediately that they were utterly exhausted and on the verge of collapse. Spracklin poured out his story and implored Langmead to help him.

Within minutes, Langmead, with the fatigued sailors in tow, was raising the alarm in the community, knocking on almost every door he passed to recruit men for the rescue attempt. Among those he collected were Christopher Baldwin, William Langmead, William Noseworthy, Christopher Mundy, and Alfred Moores. These five men, along with Langmead himself, would play a dominant role in the events that unfolded over the next few hours.

Armed with lanterns and ropes, the men, led by Spracklin, hurried back toward the sea and the wounded *Waterwitch*.

"Sounds like they came ashore in Horrid Gulch," Langmead suggested to Moores as they made their way toward the cliffs.

"Yes," Moores replied. "I believe you're right." Then as an afterthought, he added, "They couldn't have picked a worse spot."

That, indeed, was the case. Horrid Gulch, aptly named, is a narrow inlet just northeast of Pouch Cove that is bounded by a 600-foot sheer precipice on the north and a 500-foot cliff on the south that is not quite as steep yet still extremely treacherous. The fishermen of the area always gave the gulch a wide berth because the sea thundered in there with such force that, even on the calmest of days, anyone entering ran the risk of being swept up by the inrushing tide and crushed against the rocky crag. It was on the south side of the gulch that the *Waterwitch* was grounded.

It was well after midnight when the rescue party reached the cliffs overlooking Horrid Gulch. Although they knew that the stricken schooner lay somewhere below them, in the darkness and the swirling snow, they could not pinpoint its exact location, nor, from where they stood, could they hear the cries of the marooned seamen. They hurriedly discussed their options and tried to decide the best way to proceed. Finally, Eli Langmead concluded, "There's only one way to do this. One of us has to go down to find them."

Alfred Moores, a forty-three-year-old Pouch Cove fisherman, had come to the same conclusion. He wondered who might step forward to volunteer. He was familiar with Horrid Gulch, having spent many hours of his youth roaming the cliffs between Pouch Cove and Cape St. Francis in search of berries and birds. He remembered that, as boys, he and his friends had often dared each other to venture partway down the cliff, and how, on the one occasion when he had foolishly attempted it, the dizzying sheer drop to the rocks below had prompted him to scramble back up again as quickly as he could. As a fisherman, he was familiar with the gulch from water level as well since he had to pass it every time he made his way to the fishing grounds, and he had often noted that it was probably one of the most dangerous spots on the coastline.

A large man in the prime of his life, Moores was arguably one of the strongest men there that night. His occupation and daily exposure to the elements had long since hardened him against the worst that Newfoundland seas had to offer, and when no other man stepped forward to volunteer to be lowered down over the cliff, he felt compelled to speak up. He wondered what his wife would say in the circumstances. With a family depending on him for support, he could not afford to take any unnecessary risks. Suddenly, he felt the same fear as when he'd rashly listened to the dares of his buddies years earlier. But, despite his reservations, the plight of the stranded people facing imminent death below, if indeed they hadn't already perished, was too much for him. Before he had any time to reconsider, he muttered, "I guess that'll have to be me."

A thick rope was hitched around a tree at the top of the cliff and its other end fitted around Moores' waist. Then, while a number of the other men supported the rope, he was lowered over the cliff into the swirling darkness of the night. As he swung outward, he felt his heart beating wildly in his chest, and he closed his eyes and held on tightly until he managed to get his fears in check. He prayed for strength to carry out the treacherous task he had embarked upon. He would need his full concentration, for he knew that even the slightest misstep could prove fatal. He was glad for the darkness; he couldn't see down into the terrible abyss beneath him.

He searched with his feet for a suitable route to make his descent, until he finally found a crevice in the cliff face that he thought might lead him to the ledge that he knew existed somewhere farther down. Tugging three times on the rope to signal the men to lower him, he gradually made his way downward over the precipice, trusting implicitly in his fellow rescuers to keep him from plunging to the rocks below. Eventually, his feet told him that he had reached the ledge he was seeking four hundred vertical feet from where he had started, and he felt a great sense of relief at being on solid ground again. The fact that he was in the right place was reinforced by the feeble cries from the shipwrecked people directly below him, which he now heard for the first time. In the first grey light of dawn, he could faintly see them. Sometime after Spracklin had left them, they had all miraculously been able to make their way off the vessel onto the ledge where they now huddled together, clinging for dear life to their precarious perch.

With enough light to see at last, Baldwin, Noseworthy, Mundy, and William Langmead were also lowered down the cliff to form a relay team that could assist in the rescue operation already in action. Eli Langmead stayed at the top to make sure that the rope remained firmly fastened to the tree.

Moores shouted down to the survivors to make them aware of his presence. When he had their attention, he threw down the hand rope he had brought with him. It missed on the first try and he had to haul it up again. He kept throwing it down and retrieving it until it was finally caught by one of the men below. The rope was fastened around the body of one of the survivors, a small middle-aged man named Iveny, who then cautiously began his zigzag ascent up the winding ledge. Moores kept the rope taut and pulled gently to assist the man's nervous crawl up the steep incline and shouted down encouragement and instructions to guide his progress. He had to coordinate his pulling of the rope with the pace of the man's ascent for fear of dislodging him, or indeed himself, from the narrow ledge. When, despite hesitation, Iveny finally reached the section of ledge upon which Moores stood, he took one look at the remaining section of cliff that he would have to scale and balked. Ignoring Iveny's panic, Moores fastened a second rope, one that had been passed down to him some time earlier, around the man's waist and ensured that it was firm and tight.

He then gave him the advice that he would repeat for each successive survivor: "Trust the men up there and don't look down. Use your legs to keep off a bit and just let them pull you up. There's nothing to fear."

With no other alternative, the man, supporting himself on the rope as Moores had instructed him, was hauled up. Along the way he was assisted and encouraged by Baldwin, Noseworthy, Mundy, and William Langmead in their relay positions in the crevice, and eventually arrived unharmed at the summit where he collapsed into the arms of the waiting crowd. In this manner, over a period of two hours, the remaining ten survivors of the *Waterwitch* were brought up one by one, first to the ledge where Moores was, some hundred feet above the sea, and from there pulled up the remaining four hundred feet by the strong arms of the Pouch Cove fishermen positioned at the top. None of the survivors was accustomed to such heights and the fear of falling to the rocks below was paramount in their minds. Yet they all kept coming, until only Alfred Moores himself was left down there. He was exhausted and his strength sapped from more than two hours of straining on the rope. His entire body ached. Bracing himself against the cliff face for such a long period of time as he assisted each person's ascent had left his limbs heavy and clumsy. Then, following his own advice, he too was pulled up into the welcoming and aching hands of his fellow rescuers.

By then, it was almost full daylight. The weather had abated somewhat and the sea, while still angry and dangerous, was beginning to calm down. The bodies of some of the victims could be seen tossing about in the surf at the bottom of the cliff, to be recovered later that day.

The survivors, despite the dreadful night they had spent huddled together at the bottom of Horrid Gulch, were none the worse for their harrowing experience, except for the few scrapes and bumps from being pulled up the rough cliff. Emotionally, however, they were devastated by the loss of loved ones and relatives. Many more had lost provisions and all their worldly possessions. They were brought to Pouch Cove where they were taken generously into houses and their needs catered to until arrangements could be made to have them transferred to their homes.

As might be expected, the brave fishermen of Pouch Cove who had carried out the rescue became overnight heroes in their own community, and as the details of their heroic deed were carried by newspapers and word of mouth, their fame spread to every corner of Newfoundland and Labrador. For his part in the heroic rescue, Alfred Moores would be awarded the prestigious Silver Medal of the Royal Humane Society of England. The others – Baldwin, Noseworthy, Mundy, as well as the two Langmeads – would receive bronze medals from the society for their brave actions. Later, in 1965, ninety years after the loss of the *Waterwitch*, the bravery of Alfred Moores was further commemorated with the erection of a plaque on the public highway at Pouch Cove, not far from Horrid Gulch, the scene of the heroic rescue.

The eleven people who were rescued from the wreck of the *Waterwitch* owed their deliverance to a number of factors, not the least of which is that their schooner came to rest on the south side of Horrid Gulch. If they had crashed onto the north side, rescue would have been virtually impossible. The men on board the schooner, even if they had made it from the vessel onto the cliff, could never by any stretch of the imagination have scaled the sheer vertical cliff on that side of the gulch, nor would rescue from the top of the precipice have been possible. They owed their lives to the grit and determination of Samuel Spracklin and Richard Ford who scaled the south cliff of Horrid Gulch and sought out the help that eventually resulted in their rescue. And thirdly, and foremost, they owed a monumental debt of gratitude to the courage and daring of Alfred Moores and the rest of the Pouch Cove fishermen, all of whom placed their own lives in great danger to save them. These six brave men, by their courageous deed in the early morning hours of November 29, 1875, earned for themselves an honoured place alongside the many other heroic men and women whose courage has so greatly enriched the history of Newfoundland and Labrador over the past five hundred years.

AUTHOR'S NOTE

The information inscribed on a commemorative plaque erected at Pouch Cove in 1965 differs slightly from the account of the rescue published in the December 4, 1875, edition of the St. John's newspaper, *The Courier*. The former indicates that nine people were lost when the *Waterwitch* was driven onto the rocks of Horrid Gulch, while *The Courier* states (correctly) that twelve people died in the disaster, including four women.

Those lost: Moses Spracklin, Jonathan Spracklin, William Spracklin, Elisabeth Spracklin, Amelia Spracklin, Priscella Spracklin, Samuel Wells, Richard Wells, Elias Ford, George Iveny, Solomon Taylor, Joanna Croke.

The survivors: Samuel Spracklin (captain and owner), Thomas Iveny, Henry W. Spracklin, Samuel Rowe, Henry Iveny, Samuel P. Spracklin, Thomas Noseworthy, Thomas Spracklin, William Wells, Richard Ford, George Wells, James H. Wells, William E. Spracklin.

It is also interesting to note that the plaque at Pouch Cove mentions only Alfred Moores, with no reference to the other five men who played such a crucial role in the rescue operation and who received bronze medals for their efforts, namely Eli Langmead, William Langmead, Christopher Baldwin, William Noseworthy, and Christopher Mundy.

Information for this story came from the *Encyclopedia of Newfoundland and Labrador*, edited by Joseph R. Smallwood (St. John's: Newfoundland Book Publishers Limited, 1967, 1981) as well as from *The Courier* (St. John's: December 4, 1875).

THE HANGING OF ELEANOR POWER

*S*he stumbled unto the scaffold, guided by two burly guards whose faces betrayed the distaste they held for the task they were performing. They led her to the centre of the scaffold where her hooded executioner stood waiting. Her loose flowing garment failed to hide the violent trembling of her body. She swayed once, and her guards moved quickly to prevent her from falling.

The crowd lining Water Street several rows deep watched, hushed. The hanging of a convicted criminal was a relatively common occurrence in St. John's at the time and always drew large crowds and high emotions. Sometimes outbursts of anger and slurs were hurled at the condemned with such fervour that the police were hard pressed to maintain order and keep the rowdy crowd at bay. At other times the crowd showed pity for the person being hanged while openly displaying their contempt for the Crown. Even more rarely, boisterous levity was the order of the day. The mood of the crowd usually depended on the identity of the condemned man and the particulars of his crime.

This hanging, however, was different. To see a woman on the gallows was a rare thing. None of the spectators had ever witnessed such an event. Most of them found it difficult to connect the frightened woman waiting under the noose to the heinous crime of which she had been convicted. Their silence accentuated their reservations and doubts.

Even the sheriff, John Thomas, appeared reluctant to initiate the proceedings that would send the woman to her death. Finally, with no option other than to carry out his prescribed responsibility, Thomas asked her if she had any last statement to make. A low moan gave a small voice to the stark terror she felt inside, having witnessed the hanging of her own husband only minutes earlier. The noose was fitted over her neck and after another interminable pause, the final order was given. With Thomas' pronouncement "May God have mercy on your soul," she too was sent to her doom. The trap door opened and she plunged downward. The snapping of her neck was audible to those standing nearby, and her body thrashed spasmodically at the end of the rope for several seconds before sagging into perpetual lifelessness. Eleanor Power, age unknown, had paid the ultimate price for her crime.

The execution was the final chapter in a sordid plot that had been hatched in the Powers' kitchen at Blackhead, Freshwater Bay, one late-August evening. A chance remark made there on that fateful day would unleash a tragic sequence of events that eventually culminated in the murder of a prominent St. John's citizen and the first recorded hanging of a female convict anywhere in British North America. The date was October 10, 1784, and justice in St. John's on that day was swift, merciless, and extreme.

At the time, Eleanor Power was a maid and washer-woman in the household of William Keene, Sr., a prominent St. John's import/export merchant, magistrate, and justice of the peace for the city. Keene's properties included a large house on Duckworth Street, along with business premises and a wharf on the south side of Water Street. He also owned a summer home, business premises, and another wharf nearby in Quidi Vidi Village. By all accounts, he was a successful and influential man of the time.

Eleanor Power had been employed by this man long enough to cultivate a deep dislike for him. She considered him to be overly demanding and vindictive, and, to her way of thinking, abusive and demeaning to the other domestics working for him. To Eleanor's Irish sensibilities, Keene represented everything that had kept the Irish people downtrodden and oppressed for centuries. Still, with nowhere else to turn to for money, she kept her mouth shut, trying to shield her true feelings from him as much as possible in order to maintain her position. She feared instant reprisal or dismissal should she accidentally reveal her true opinion of him.

Eleanor Power was not alone in her dislike for Keene. Her sentiments toward him, in fact, reflected those held by a large segment of the St. John's public, especially those of Irish descent who at the time comprised almost half of the city's total population. Keene, as a public official, was well known for the excessive sentences he routinely meted out for what were considered mostly minor crimes. There were many enemies and detractors in and around St. John's who, having experienced Keene's form of justice firsthand, would have gladly done him serious bodily harm if given the opportunity. Eleanor Power was far from being the only person in the area to feel at least some degree of enmity toward the man.

One evening in late August, unbeknownst to her and possibly without any malice intended, Eleanor Power sowed the seeds of her own demise by disclosing to her husband, Robert Power, and a number of other men the fact that Keene kept a large sum of money in his house in Quidi Vidi Village, and that she knew where he kept it. Her fateful words were uttered in her home in Blackhead where her husband and the others were drinking, slowly becoming intoxicated in the gathering dusk, as they often did. Whether her comments were intended to instigate the events that subsequently unfolded or whether they were merely passing conversation is unclear, but they immediately piqued the interest of Robert Power and his companions.

"How much?" they wanted to know, to which she replied that it was at least a thousand pounds, and that she had watched Keene take it out and count it once when he didn't know she was around. She added that he kept it in a chest under the stairs, hidden under linens and other such household items.

Keene and his money remained the main topic of discussion for the rest of the evening, during which someone raised the notion of stealing it from him. The suggestion, which may have initially been made in jest, took root and quickly gained momentum. Before the night was over, a conspiracy was minted to pilfer the old man's money. A thousand pounds, even when divided among all of them, was more money than any of them had ever seen in their lifetimes.

The conspirators met again in the Powers' house during the next three or four evenings to finalize the details of their plot. By that time the group had grown to a considerable size, now comprising nine members including Edmund McGuire, Matthew Halleran, Paul MacDonald, Lawrence Lumley, John Moody, Dennis Hawkins, and John Munhall, in addition to Eleanor and Robert Power, all of whom were of Irish descent and some of whom were soldiers stationed in the fort at nearby Cape Spear. In that short time, McGuire had established himself as the ringleader of the group.

One night in the first week of September, the gang made its move. At that point another man, Nicholas Tobin, was drawn through necessity into the plot. Tobin operated a ferry service between Freshwater Bay and St. John's. He was needed to transport the others across the five-mile expanse of rough water to the scene of the intended robbery. In return he would receive a share of the spoils. When they arrived in Quidi Vidi Village around midnight, the wharf was still busy with a number of fishermen at work despite the late hour, cleaning and salting down an exceptionally large catch of cod from that day. There being no indication that the fishermen would be leaving any time soon, the gang decided to abandon their plan that night and return at another time.

Three nights later they tried again. This time, to their chagrin, they found that Keene had guests. Two large vessels were berthed at his private wharf, and several lights burned in his house nearby. For a second time, they were forced to abort their plan.

Finally, on September 9, they made their third attempt. This time they were armed, although they did not intend to harm Keene. They only wanted his money. Two muskets, carried by Robert Power and Halleran, and a broken scythe blade carried by McGuire comprised their arsenal. Arriving again at midnight, they forced their way into Keene's house, where Eleanor Power led them to the chest under the stairs where she had witnessed Keene handling his money. The old man did not awaken, and the group was able to carry the chest away without any alarm being raised. The chest was heavy for its size; those carrying it believed that perhaps it contained even more than the thousand pounds that Eleanor Power had told them about.

They halted a short distance away from the house in a spot where they felt they would be safe from spying eyes. When they broke the chest open, however, they found to their dismay that the chest did not contain any money at all. Instead, they stared at several bottles of liquor. Frustrated, some of them now turned on Eleanor Power and accused her of leading them on a fool's errand. Fearing for her safety, she insisted that she had seen Keene's money just as she had told them but he must have moved it. Then she suggested that it might still be in the house, probably in another chest that she knew he kept under his bed.

The group remained there some time, squabbling among themselves, drinking Keene's liquor, and gradually becoming drunk. Then, drunk, the fuming McGuire announced that he was going to return to the house and have another try. The group was split on the idea, some, despite their drunken state, opposed, suddenly fearful of the consequences. McGuire insisted that he was going anyway and anyone who wanted to come with him was welcome. Those who didn't wouldn't receive a single farthing. Finally, McGuire, Robert Power, and Halleran returned to the Keene residence. Power stood guard outside and around one o'clock in the morning the other two men entered the house once again – for the final time.

They quickly located Keene's sleeping chamber and the chest underneath his bed. As they were removing the chest, however, Keene awoke and began to scream for help. McGuire, panic-stricken, stabbed the old man twice with the scythe blade, while Halleran struck Keene in the head with the butt of his musket and placed a quilt over his head to suffocate him until his body lay still on the bed. Then the assailants fled, taking the chest with them. It would be another ten days before Keene succumbed to his injuries, most likely dying of an infection caused by McGuire's rusted scythe blade.

The authorities were not long in identifying the perpetrators of the foul deed, for the plot was an ill-kept secret that was broadly known throughout Freshwater Bay. All ten were arrested shortly afterward and brought to trial.

Nicholas Tobin, hoping to save his own skin, immediately turned state's evidence. Under oath at the trial, he confessed everything, revealing the details of the plot, the names and roles of the participants, the two aborted attempts to rob Keene's money, and the final September 9 botched entry of Keene's house and his subsequent murder. He named McGuire and Halleran as the actual murderers, and Robert Power as their accomplice. He also implicated Eleanor Power as the instigator of the whole affair. For providing this evidence, the charge against Tobin was dropped.

The other nine were found guilty. Those not directly involved in the actual slaying of Keene, including Eleanor Power, argued that they should have been charged only with break and entry, not murder – not even robbery. The court disagreed, and all were sentenced to be hanged for their crime.

The executions of Eleanor and Robert Power were scheduled for October 10, 1784, near Keene's own wharf on Water Street, and were carried out as ordered. Both of their bodies were buried near the execution site in keeping with the custom of the day.

By a strange twist that is difficult to comprehend, the death sentences of the others, including the actual murderers, McGuire and Halleran, were almost immediately commuted by Governor Hugh

26   Bonfoy. In fact, the remaining seven men were later pardoned and
freed altogether.

Except for her involvement in the Keene affair, little factual
information is known about Eleanor Power. There is some suggestion
that she was born and raised on the southeast coast of Ireland, perhaps
in Wexford, Waterford, or New Ross. English ships put in to such
ports in southeastern Ireland on a regular basis each year to deliver
fish from Newfoundland and to ship back cargo, including thousands
of Irish immigrants. There, the transplanted Irish served as a source
of cheap labour for the bustling enterprises of Britain's oldest colony.
If Eleanor Power was indeed from that area, she undoubtedly would
have endured a hungry childhood of hardship. As a young woman, she
would most likely have immigrated to Newfoundland, indenturing
herself, in return for her passage, as a servant for a period of at least
two years to some wealthy St. John's citizen, perhaps William Keene,
Sr., himself.

The fact that she and her husband lived in Blackhead, a small
fishing community near St. John's, suggests that Robert Power was a
fisherman. It may also be inferred, because she herself was employed in
St. John's and had to make the journey to the city by boat on a regular
basis, that Eleanor Power's indenture to Keene may not yet have
elapsed. It is not known if she had any children.

While specific information about Eleanor Power's life is vague or
unavailable, one fact is abundantly clear. Her punishment, in relation
to all the others who were involved in the plot, was extremely
harsh. It appears that she was made a scapegoat for the death of
Keene, and that her hanging was meant to serve as a deterrent to the
Irish population of St. John's and the surrounding area, which was
well known for its rowdiness. A message greatly reinforced by the
unprecedented hanging of a woman.

It is clear that Eleanor Power was singled out for an unjust and
excessive punishment, especially in light of the fact that Keene's actual

murderers went scot-free in the end. The fact that she herself had refused to participate in the last and fatal entry of the Keene residence was totally ignored by those who judged her. With the dubious distinction of being the first woman to be hanged in British North America, her body still lies today in an unmarked grave somewhere near the intersection of Water Street and Prescott Street in St. John's east end, where countless vehicle drivers and pedestrians pass over her grave every day unaware that she ever existed.

AUTHOR'S NOTE

The factors which prompted Governor Bonfoy's decision to pardon and free all of the participants in the plot except Eleanor and Robert Power are unclear. His decision may have been influenced by the groundswell of protest from the large and volatile Irish population of the area at the time. Their outrage against this unheard of hanging of a female was violent and extensive, particularly with respect to a woman deemed by many to be undeserving of the extreme punishment she received.

This story is based on information from *The Oldest City* by Paul O'Neill (St. John's: Boulder Publications, 1975) and the *Encyclopedia of Newfoundland and Labrador*, edited by Joseph R. Smallwood (St. John's: Newfoundland Book Publishers Limited, 1967, 1981).

TWO
BROTHERS

ohn Rousell laid his knife on the splitting table, wiped the sweat
from his forehead, and stood back to survey his handiwork.
He was satisfied by what he saw. The weir,[2] now filled with
salmon, was the product of almost four months of hard labour,
back-breaking toil that had sometimes seemed unbearable and unending.
Each rock and log, some of which had been fetched from a considerable
distance, had been painstakingly placed in position one by one until a
large deep pool had finally been created at the mouth of the river. It was
there that the Atlantic salmon making their annual migration back to
their spawning grounds were now trapped, waiting to be caught, gutted,
and salted by Rousell at his leisure. A large percentage of these fish would
be able to breach the weir to continue their journey upriver to lay their
eggs, thus maintaining the salmon population of the river for future years.
Enough, however, would linger in the coolness of the weir long enough to
enable Rousell to take as many as he wanted.

Rousell had chosen his location well. This river, situated on the
southwest corner of Hall's Bay on the north coast of Newfoundland, was
perfect for his purpose. The teeming mass of salmon in the weir was proof
of the wisdom of his selection. As he rested briefly from his work, he felt
a glowing sense of accomplishment, something which had eluded him for

---

[2] A weir is a fence or enclosure set in a waterway for the taking of fish,
usually located at the mouth of a river.

much of his life. From the moment he first arrived in Hall's Bay, he had not only recognized the salmon potential of the place but had been struck by its beauty. He was one of only a handful of residents in the area at that time.

The crude hut he had hastily erected when he first arrived was the only jarring note in his surroundings. It was a rough structure known as a "leaning tilt" whose walls consisted of vertical tree trunks laid side by side aslant against a log frame upon which rested more horizontal logs, stuffed with boughs and moss, to form a roof. A gap in one of the walls, covered by an animal hide, served as a door, and a small hole in the roof allowed the smoke to escape from the tilt's interior. He knew he would have to construct something much better before he could bring Mary out here to live with him. That was a task he planned to undertake in the fall, after he had delivered his summer's catch of salmon to Exploits.

He had started the weir with his brother Tom. They had initially been partners in the enterprise, but after the first few weeks Tom had lost interest and wandered off into the interior, reappearing thereafter at odd intervals, and then for only a day or two at a time. Of the two, John was the stable one, and a fisherman. Tom was a roamer, a furrier driven by the desire to live alone and try to survive by his own wits in the wilderness far removed from the social fabric of the region. Neither of them had been deterred from coming to Hall's Bay by its grisly history. Five previous white settlers, presumably the first in the area, had been slaughtered by Beothuk Indians, beheaded, and their heads left on stakes as a warning to other white men to stay away. That, however, was long in the past. The Rousells were not intimidated by the story or, indeed, even gave it much thought. They were both strapping men in the prime of their lives and fully confident in their ability to face whatever might confront them. In any event, the presence of Beothuk in this area was now a rare occurrence as the major portion of the Beothuk population had long since been driven inland where it was believed they congregated mainly around Red Indian Lake.

On that day the Red Indians were far removed from John Rousell's mind. His brief rest over, he returned to his work. Dipping a large salmon from the weir and placing it on the table, he proceeded to gut it. A slash across the gills and a long incision along the fish's underbelly quickly exposed its innards, which he removed with one efficient motion before tossing the processed fish into the tub with the others. The whole procedure had taken only a few seconds. Long practise had perfected his technique to the point where he could do it repeatedly and automatically without much thought. He dipped his net into the water to get another one. It was then that he realized he wasn't alone. On the bank of the river, not more than fifty feet away, stood three individuals. He recognized immediately that they were Beothuk, two male adults and a boy. They were regarding him intently.

The men were tall, much taller than he was, and well proportioned. Their fierce appearance was heightened by the red ochre with which they had smeared their faces and bodies. They were armed with bows and arrows, and knives and hatchets hung from their belts. They had him cornered. Fear rooted Rousell to the spot. For a fleeting moment he thought about making a dash for his long-gun, which rested, primed and ready, against the tilt – seventy feet away. He knew, however, that he would receive an arrow in the back before he had taken more than a couple of steps. He was no match for them. They had all the advantages.

As he stood there waiting for the Beothuk to make their move, his fear and dread gave way to an overwhelming sadness that swept over him and blotted out everything else. He was going to die. His death would undoubtedly be a brutal one, yet his thoughts at that moment were of the life and the undone things he would be leaving behind, and of Mary waiting for him back in Exploits. She might never know what had happened to him.

Then he did something which he could never quite explain afterwards. It was a simple act, done instinctively without premeditation, a desperate last straw by a doomed man. He took the still writhing salmon from the dip-net and tossed it onto the grassy bank of the river in the vicinity of the Indians. He gestured toward the salmon-filled weir – a clear invitation to the Beothuk to take whatever they wanted. For what seemed like an eternity the Indians did not respond. Finally, one of the men nodded to the boy, who immediately sprang to retrieve the salmon before it could wriggle back into the water. A few seconds later, miraculously, the threesome melted back into the woods, leaving the shaken Rousell awash with relief – and still alive.

He clutched the splitting table to try to steady his trembling knees and shaking body, resisting the urge to sink onto the soft ground. He was exhausted. The encounter had drained him, and his perspiration-soaked body wanted only to rest for a while. Finally he made his way to the tilt, where he reached into its uppermost regions and extracted an earthen jug and its precious contents of dark rum. As he drank, the fiery liquid coursing through his body gave him comfort. He knew that soon the trembling would cease and his body would return to normal. He stayed in the tilt all that day and into the night, his long-gun never more than an arm's reach away, until finally, despite his efforts to stay awake, he fell asleep and did not reawaken until late the following morning.

During the next two days his daily routine gradually returned to its normal state – almost. He resumed his work with one eye on the task at hand and the other on the nearby woods, ever watchful, with his long-gun never far from his side. Things would never be quite the same again. He was on constant alert now and aware for the first time of his vulnerability in this sparsely populated area.

And then his brother showed up. Tom Rousell arrived just before nightfall bearing a brace of rabbits which he and John quickly cooked into a hearty stew. When they had eaten, they retired to the tilt and the rum jug once again descended from its lofty position. There, in the dimly lit interior, John related to Tom his experience with the Beothuk three days earlier.

"I wish I'd been here," Tom offered. "I would have had those dirty savages. They wouldn't have gotten away from me."

"Well," John replied, "there was no real harm done, I suppose. I'm still alive to tell the tale, although I must admit I got the fright of my life. Anyway, if they come back again I'll have my gun ready."

The two brothers sipped rum, getting quietly drunk, and continued to talk into the night. Then, in the early hours of the morning, when he was quite intoxicated, Tom made a horrific admission.

"John," he slurred, "I've got something to tell you." He paused, as if reconsidering what he was about to say. Then he committed himself. "I've already killed a few of them, you know."

"A few of what?" his startled brother asked.

"Savages, Red Indians," Tom said. "Five in all."

John was incredulous. "Why? When?"

"The first one was an accident. I came across two of them when we surprised each other in a clearing in the woods. They weren't aware of my presence nor I of theirs. They were armed and one of them started to come at me so I shot him. Blew the bugger's brains out, I did. The other one took off before I could reload. That was the beginning. Then, later, I was making my way through the woods one day when I noticed some movement in a bush that I didn't think was right. So I moved in close and blasted into the bush, and sure enough, another one of the dirty devils was in there. Looked like a boy, probably trying to hide from me."

"And the others?" John asked, dreading the answer.

"Well, by then I suspected they knew me and would be on the lookout for me. So I had to be extra careful. I took to following a different route along my trap-line as I figured that was where they might be waiting to ambush me. But I fooled them. And one day when I arrived to check one of my traps, there were three of them trying to take out a beaver that was caught. I chose my position well, where I would have time to reload before they could get to me.

"So I waited until the right moment, and I let go. It was a long shot, but I dropped one stone dead. The others came at me but I had time to reload and I got another one of the buggers. I was pretty sure that some of my shot hit the third one as well but he ran off. But he left a trail of blood that I could follow and pretty soon I came upon him. He was almost gone so I finished him off too. Got all three, I did. And then I got out of there," he said. "Pass me the jug."

Tom Rousell took a final swig of rum, laid back upon the boughs that served as his bed, and, within seconds, was fast asleep.

Sleep for John, however, would not come. As drunk as he was, he was horrified by what his brother had told him. He had always known that Tom was rough and ready, but tonight he had witnessed a dark side of his brother that he had never seen before.

Two days later, Tom left again. After his disclosure in the tilt that night, neither he nor John had mentioned the matter again. John thought briefly, perhaps wishfully, that his brother might have made it all up. He knew in his heart, however, that that was not the case. It was all true. A tension that had never existed before now separated them. For the first time in their lives, they were uncomfortable in each other's presence. John was glad to see his brother go.

John continued to do his work each day, albeit without the energy and enthusiasm that had previously marked his working hours. He was preoccupied with his brother's wanton slaying of the Beothuk. He couldn't reconcile Tom's actions with the carefree sibling he'd grown up with and had looked after for much of his life. He wondered when and why Tom had changed so much. He could understand him killing in self-defence, as perhaps might be argued in the slaying of the first man, but certainly not the rest. That was murder, pure and simple. John was aware that the killing of Beothuk had been legislated in the early 1800s to be a criminal act punishable by the full force of the law. If found out, he knew that his brother might indeed have to forfeit his own life.

About three weeks after Tom left, John was jolted out of his usual early morning sluggishness when he emerged from the tilt to discover that the same three Beothuk, the two men and the boy, had reappeared. They were waist-deep in the weir spearing up salmon. They looked his way but did not pause in their activity. For a fleeting moment, John contemplated firing at them. Then he remembered that they had spared his life when they so easily could have killed him, as well as his open invitation to them to help themselves to his salmon. So he quickly dismissed the notion. Shortly thereafter the Beothuk, having taken all they wanted, left.

By the end of August, John had stockpiled as much salted salmon as he could transport to the fish merchant in Exploits,[3] some forty miles away. Still, he hesitated to go and postponed his departure as long as possible because he had not heard from Tom since his last visit, and was worried. Finally, knowing that if he delayed much longer he ran the risk of losing his summer's catch in the hot weather, he set out. Closely following the coastline all the way lest he run into foul weather or some other peril in his small boat, he eventually made his way to Exploits without incident.

He remained there for almost a month, disposing of his catch and making plans with Mary for their future. Then, in late September, he set out once again for Hall's Bay to work on the tilt to get it ready for Mary. She had agreed to come back there with him the following spring.

His return journey by boat landed him in Hall's Bay two days later. The uneventful trip and calm weather, and his time spent with Mary, had restored his sense of contentment and purpose, and as he pulled his boat upon the bank at the mouth of the river, he felt energized and ready for the work ahead. His peace of mind, however, was about to be shattered.

---

[3] During the time period of this story, the settlement of Exploits was the major centre of the Notre Dame Bay salmon fishery and fur trade. It was there that John Peyton, Sr., and his family initially established and operated their extensive salmon and furrier enterprises.

As soon as he set foot ashore, he knew something was wrong. His instincts told him that something dreadful was about to happen. It was a sensation unlike anything he had ever experienced before. And then he saw it, not more than twenty feet from the tilt. There, impaled on a stake, was his brother's head, its sightless milky eyes staring vacantly into the distance. Close by, Tom's headless body rested on the ground. The bloated corpse still showed the mutilation that had been inflicted upon it at the time of death. The younger Rousell had clearly experienced the most horrific death imaginable.

John Rousell had difficulty fathoming the gruesome scene. Vomit welled up in his mouth and spewed onto the ground at the sight of his brother's decapitated body. His own body heaved uncontrollably and bitter bile burned his throat. His knees gave out and he fell to the ground. He was filled with disbelief, revulsion, and rage, and for one of the few times in his life he felt utterly helpless. And then he broke down and cried. He wept bitterly and long, until no more tears would come and, numbed, he finally rose to his feet to do what he had to do. He cursed himself over and over for having left the area without first knowing that his brother was alive and safe.

He buried Tom by the side of the river. He did not mark the grave because he feared the Beothuk might return and desecrate it. Then he got back in his boat and returned to Exploits, leaving his intended work on the tilt undone.

That winter was the worst of his life. He was haunted by guilt and the image of his brother's mutilated body. He could not shake from his mind the grisly scene that had confronted him at the river. Indeed, it would remain with him for the rest of his life. He abandoned his plans to return to Hall's Bay and the life he had planned there for Mary and himself. He never wanted to see the place again.

The period from January to March was one of the most severe in many years. Heavy snow came early and covered the ground to a considerable depth, making normal movement difficult and in some cases impossible. Winds pounded the north coast of Newfoundland for weeks on end, and John's energies, like those of most of the area's population, were expended in keeping himself and Mary warm and alive. Little else mattered. Time passed at an excruciatingly slow pace as the long nights and short days blended into an unbroken period of cold misery for all. With little else to occupy his time, the circumstances of Tom's death played heavily on his mind and left John depressed and melancholic for much of the time.

John Rousell, however, was nothing if not resolute and persevering, and as spring finally approached, he made a conscious effort to shake himself from his depression and to consider his options for the future. He and Mary talked at great length, until gradually, despite what had happened there, the thought of returning to Hall's Bay became entrenched in his mind. When he broached the subject with her, she, knowing how much he desired to go back, agreed to go with him even though the tilt was all he had to offer for her living accommodations. They would work on it together.

In early May, John's boat once again grounded onto the bank of the river, and he and Mary stepped ashore to begin their new life in Hall's Bay. She, like John, was immediately entranced by the beauty of the area. He showed her where Tom was buried, and she wept silently over his grave until he took her by the hand and gently led her away. Then he took her inside the tilt. As he expected, she was not impressed and let him know in no uncertain terms that cleaning it up and improving it would have to be their utmost priority.

John and Mary spent their first summer there, operating the salmon weir and preparing the site for their new home. In the fall they built a proper house for themselves and laid out a vegetable garden for planting the following spring. They would spend the rest of their lives there at the mouth of the river, raising a family in the process. In the early years they occasionally caught glimpses of tall red-skinned strangers helping themselves to a few salmon from the weir. With the passage of time, however, the periodic appearances of the Beothuk became fewer and fewer until they eventually failed to materialize at all. By then the Beothuk people were all but extinct. The

remaining handful of this race had been pushed far back into the
interior of Newfoundland by the ever encroaching presence of white
settlers in the area, and within a few short years they would cease to
exist at all.

It is clear that the Beothuk who had frequented the Hall's Bay
area knew the Rousells, and in all likelihood understood that they were
blood brothers. It is obvious, too, that they differentiated between the
two men, recognizing the inherent goodness of John Rousell as well as
the true nature of his brother Tom. Their retribution against the
latter had been swift and merciless, while John Rousell and his family,
on the other hand, were never threatened or, with the exception of
the occasional loss of a few salmon, bothered in any way. It might
even be argued that the deliverance of Tom's body to the weir by
the Beothuk had been an act of kindness on their part. It enabled John
to give his brother a proper burial, for the Beothuk themselves had a
great belief in *Theehone*, the afterlife. Mary and John lived out their
days on the river in Hall's Bay in peace and contentment, secure in
their knowledge that they and their children were safe from any form
of hostility from their aboriginal neighbours.

AUTHOR'S NOTE

The Rousell brothers, Tom and John, are also referred to by the
names Rowsell and Roue in James P. Howley's *The Beothucks or
Red Indians* (Cambridge: Cambridge University Press, 1915).

It is not known for sure how many Beothuk Tom Rousell
actually killed in his time, but his reputation as an "Indian
Killer" was well known throughout Notre Dame Bay. There
is no doubt that he, and a number of others like him,
contributed significantly to the eventual eradication of the
Beothuk race. Starvation and white man's diseases, tuberculosis in particular, as well as the ongoing hostility with the
Mi'kmaq, did the rest.

PIUS CARROLL
GOES SWILING

*F*rom her kitchen window, Bridie Carroll watched her son marching up the lane and could tell by his resolute stride that he had something on his mind. Pius was coming home with a purpose.

She wouldn't have to wait long to find out what it was. As soon as he opened the door, he called out, "Mother, you'll never guess what I've done now."

Before she had time to open her mouth, he blurted out, "I'm going swiling.[4] I've got a berth with Captain Dickie."

Bridie was floored. Her son often tried to surprise her and keep her in suspense while he made her guess whatever it was he was up to. Usually it was something trivial or relatively unimportant. Certainly nothing of this magnitude. Her every instinct told her to tell him no, he couldn't go, that he was too young and she needed him here with her. Yet she held her tongue. After all, her son, at seventeen, was a man, or almost. Perhaps there was another way.

"Oh, Pius," she started, "you're just fooling me, aren't you? I'd be so worried about you out there in that dreadful weather. It's so dangerous. Every year men are lost, you know, and what for? Surely not the few paltry coppers they get out of it. They're just pawns of the merchants,

---

[4] Swiling is an old Newfoundland term for sealing.

that's all they are."

"Don't worry," Pius countered. "It won't be dangerous for me. I'm only going to be the cook's helper, that's all, and I won't even be out on the ice. I'll be on the steamer the whole time getting the sealers their meals."

Then he added, "Captain Dickie told me that I'll be earning a half share and all the flippers I can sell when we get back."

"But you don't have any clothes warm enough for going to the ice, and we haven't got the money to buy you any. You'll freeze to death."

"Don't fret about that either, Mother." The boy laughed. "I won't be cold. If anything, it will probably be too hot for me down there in the galley with the stove going full tilt all the time. I'll be leaving in three days time."

"And what about me?" Bridie said. "How will I manage here by myself all that time?" She hated herself for saying it, yet added, "It's a hard time of the year, you know."

"It'll only be for four or five weeks," he told her. "And I'll have everything done for you before I go. You won't have to lift your hand to a thing while I'm gone, I promise you.

"Anyway," he added, "I've got to run over and tell Mavis. Isn't it grand? To be able to do something I've always wanted to do, and be paid for it in the bargain."

After he left, Bridie sat at the kitchen table and tried to come to grips with the idea that Pius would be going away. She just couldn't stand the thought of him leaving, even for only a few weeks. Worse still was the fact that he would be going to the ice with all its inherent risks. She was ashamed for having tried to make him feel guilty, but she still hadn't discounted the notion of trying to get him to change his mind. Maybe Mavis, his young girlfriend, would persuade him not to go, although Bridie knew in her heart that nothing the girl might say would deter Pius.

Bridie slept very little that night. She couldn't focus on anything else. Pius was her only child, and the two of them had lived alone together for the past twelve years, since her husband passed away. The boy had been only five at the time. Despite her loss and her occasional loneliness, their little house at the extreme end of the Lower Battery, the closest one to the ocean outside the St. John's narrows, had been a haven of contentment and security for her and her son. Pius' going now was a strong indication that he would be leaving her for good sometime, and the thought devastated her. He was the purpose of her life. Little else mattered.

Bridie had prayed for her son every night since he was born. Whenever he was out of her sight she always wondered where he was and what he was up to. Even now, despite the fact that Pius was a young man, she could never go to sleep, no matter what the hour, until she heard him come in and knew that he was safe. And tonight she prayed again, intensifying her prayers as she sought divine intervention. Finally she slept, and when she awoke in the morning she was reconciled to the fact that her son would be going swiling.

Pius, true to his word, spent the next two days ensuring that his mother would be well looked after while he was gone. He sawed, cleaved, and stored junks until he was certain there was enough firewood to keep her warm through his absence. He brought fresh water until the two large barrels out in the back porch were filled, and he put his hand to every other task and chore he could think of to make his mother's life a little easier. He even had the foresight to pay a visit to his Uncle Bill in the west end of St. John's to ask him to look in on his mother every now and then.

On Saturday morning, seventeen-year-old Pius, clad in his flannel shirt, long underwear, twill pants, canvas windbreaker, and rubber knee-boots, was among the large group of sealers crowding the rail of the *Raven* as she steamed slowly toward the narrows to begin her voyage to the Front, the large ice-fields off the northeast coast of Newfoundland. Shortly after Captain Dickie had given the order to ship anchor, Pius caught a glimpse of his house and was sure he saw his mother standing out in the garden waving to him. He waved back, unaware of the heartache he was causing.

For Pius, it was the beginning of a great adventure. Although he was busy down in the galley doing the countless chores assigned to him by the cook, he nevertheless found time to pop up on deck every now and then to take in the sights. The dipping and rolling of the vessel as she steamed along and the wind on his face were exhilarating, while the wake of the ship let him know that with each passing minute he was travelling farther away from home than he had ever been before. He revelled in every minute of his new experience.

For two days the *Raven* plodded on toward her destination, doing a steady eight knots. It wasn't until they passed Cape Freels, the headland that separates Bonavista Bay and Notre Dame Bay, that they began to encounter random patches of broken ice, the first they had seen since leaving St. John's. Having come more than three hundred miles without obstruction, they now had to proceed more cautiously. The ice, however, was not yet dense enough to seriously impede their progress.

Steering almost due north from that point, Captain Dickie told the sealers that they would probably have to steam another two hundred miles or more before they reached the large ice-fields which, at that time of the year, crept slowly southward from the polar cap, hopefully bringing with them the thousands of whitecoats whelped only days earlier. Another day saw them in thicker ice and a few seals were spotted but not enough to warrant stopping. Finally, on the fifth day, the lookouts reported a large seal herd to the starboard and Captain Dickie announced, "B'ys, it's time to go to work. We're in the fat."

The seal hunt had begun. For the next fourteen days, with the exception of Sundays, the sealers, organized in watches of a dozen men or more, were dispatched to various locations on the ice to harvest as many seals as possible before the *Raven* came back to collect them before dark. At first light each morning, the men, armed with sealing gaffs and hauling ropes and having been fed a good breakfast, slipped over the side of the vessel onto the ice to begin their day's work. Pius watched them leave and wished that he was going with them.

When they returned at dusk, the bloodied sealers were ravenously hungry and the mountains of salted pork, figgy duffs, and gallons of hot tea that Pius had helped prepare invariably disappeared in short order. As busy as he was, this was Pius' favourite time of the day. He loved to listen to the sealers talking as they ate, and to hear them boast about their exploits out on the ice. Day after day, he was enraptured by the yarns they told and the ridiculous lengths they went to in striving to outdo each other. Pius resolved that before the voyage was over he would go out onto the ice with them.

By the fifteenth day, the hold of the *Raven* was almost filled, and Captain Dickie announced, "Another good day or two, b'ys, and we'll be heading for home."

Pius knew he didn't have much time left. Tomorrow, he determined, would be his day.

He was up well before the sealers the next morning to help get breakfast ready before they went to work. Afterward, he observed the watches as they left the ship one by one until only one remained. When that group dropped over the side and proceeded outward in single file, Pius, unobserved, went with them. He carried with him a gaff and a rope he had hidden away the previous night. Keeping to the rear to avoid detection, he was on his way to realizing his dream.

Pius had walked almost a half mile before he was discovered. Abram Bussey, the watch leader, was livid and ordered him to return to the steamer. Pius' assertion that Captain Dickie had given him permission to come, a blatant lie, held no sway with Bussey – at least not at first. The boy's persistence, however, eventually created a niggling doubt in the watch leader's mind, and with the threat, "If I find out you've lied to me I'll skin you alive when we get back," Pius was grudgingly permitted to tag along.

The weather, although overcast and cold, was calm and the air was still, perhaps eerily so. Pius felt no discomfort despite the scanty clothing he wore. The effort of keeping up with the others, in fact, had left him sweating slightly, and the feel of the sweat on his body felt good. He was looking forward to killing his share of whitecoats.

Within the space of two hours, the tranquility of the morning would be transformed into a maelstrom, and the ice-field would become a death trap. The first indicators were icy blasts from the northwest that sent the temperature plummeting. As the wind veered farther to the north, isolated snowflakes materialized and rapidly escalated into driving snow that stung the men's faces and reduced visibility to almost zero. At times they could barely see each other even though they were only a few feet apart. The temperature continued to drop, and the men knew they were in trouble. Bussey assembled the others. "B'ys, we're in for a hard time until the skipper comes for us," he told them. "There's nothing to do but bide here and wait."

Then he cautioned, "You've got to keep moving about. You can't stop or you might freeze. I'm sure the skipper will get here as soon as he can."

Even as he said it, he, along with most of the others, knew that Captain Dickie might have difficulty locating them. They were not where the captain had dropped them off. For the seals which had been plentiful in that area the previous day had since disappeared, and Bussey, as watch master, had made the decision to search for them elsewhere. Consequently, they were at least three miles south of where the captain would expect them to be.

The storm raged all morning. At first, the stranded sealers mounded up snow to provide a barricade against the wind, but their efforts were futile and the snow blew away as quickly as they piled it up. Thus exposed, they had no other way to shelter themselves and keep warm. The more experienced among them bemoaned the fact that they didn't have any seal carcasses, for the oily bodies would burn efficiently and provide heat. As well, the stacked carcasses could serve as a windbreak. Unfortunately, the men were left to their own devices. Their only option was to keep shuffling around to keep the blood flowing in their freezing bodies.

Six miles away, Captain Dickie was worried. As soon as the storm erupted, he had gone to collect his men. By noon, all but Bussey's watch had been gathered in and were safely on board. He was sure, despite the driving snow, that he had gone to the correct location, to the area where he had left them. He ordered that the horn be blown continuously to let Bussey and the others know that he was in the vicinity, and sent men out onto the ice to look for them. After an hour of fruitless searching, he knew he would have to look elsewhere. He turned eastward, concluding that the sealers must be trying to make their own way back to the steamer. He did not know that Pius was among those he was searching for.

By mid-afternoon the storm had intensified, and the plight of the stranded men worsened. With darkness rapidly approaching, some of them began to lose hope. Some ceased their walking and sank onto the ice, too tired to continue and resigned to whatever fate might now befall them. Most of them now realized that their survival depended on Captain Dickie locating them, and prayed that the skipper would find them before it was too late.

Pius felt colder than he'd ever felt before. The shirt and windbreaker he wore offered virtually no protection against the storm, and the fierce northern wind pierced his body mercilessly without letup. He tried to keep moving, but he knew he was freezing to death on his feet. He was so numb and stiff he could barely move his arms and legs, and each step in the blinding snowstorm required enormous effort. With darkness now descending, he was frightened, and his mother's words about men being lost on the ice each year rang loudly in his mind. He was also afraid of what Abram Bussey might do to him if he stopped. He had reached the point, however, where he could carry on no longer and, despite Bussey's order, slumped down on the ice to rest. As snow drifted around him and covered his exposed body, he eventually drifted into unconsciousness.

Five hundred miles away, in her bed in St. John's, Bridie Carroll worried about the storm buffeting her house. Her windows rattled so violently she feared they would break, and gusts of wind shook the dwelling so viciously she thought it must surely topple from its foundation. She couldn't remember a storm of this intensity in many years. Yet, amidst all this, Pius was foremost on her mind.

She couldn't sleep. I'm just tormenting myself, she thought. This storm is just around here. It's probably as calm as a summer's day up there.

Still, no matter how she tried to reassure herself, Bridie couldn't put herself at ease. She lay in her bed as the storm continued to punish her house as she prayed over and over for Pius' safety. Finally, around three o'clock in the morning, the winds abated and the sounds of the storm ceased. It was then, there in the darkness of her bedroom as she was finally beginning to doze off, that a noise caught her attention: footsteps on the stairs. She sat up in her bed. Someone was coming up, and then opening and shutting a door – the door to Pius' room.

She wasn't afraid. She left her bed and went to her son's room. She opened the door and entered. She knelt at his empty bedside and prayed more fervently than ever before. At seven o'clock in the morning, as the first light of day filtered through the room's tiny curtained window, she finally arose. She returned to her own bed and slept as deeply and as untroubled as she had when she was a small child.

Pius, now encased in his icy cocoon, was oblivious to the storm raging about him. He was unaware that men were perishing all around him, succumbing one by one to their dire circumstances. He was in his own bed at the top of the stairs, yet he was freezing, and he had no blankets to cover himself and make himself warm. He couldn't move, and didn't know what to do. Then he heard her coming, as he knew she would. She came to his bedside and covered him with a thick heated quilt, then she bent down and kissed him gently on his forehead. She left, and warmth was restored to Pius' frozen body.

Sometime later he was jolted by the prolonged blaring of a ship's horn. Must be a steamer coming in through the St. John's narrows, he thought. But why is she blowing like that? Must be some kind of trouble on board.

Then he heard voices, muffled voices and words he couldn't understand. They came closer, until he distinctly heard a familiar voice say, "That makes seven. Poor devils, they perished where they stood. They didn't stand a chance. At least there's five still alive. Let's get them aboard first and then come back for the dead ones."

The voices receded. Then Pius felt something nudge his body and another voice calling out, "Here, what's this?"

He felt hands pulling his mother's quilt off him. He reached up to tug it back, opened his eyes, and looked directly into the compassionate face of Captain Dickie. He sat up, then slowly rose to his feet, his ice-encrusted clothing frozen to his body. His rescuers were astonished. How could a youngster clad in only a canvas windbreaker survive when grown men dressed in much warmer clothing had been frozen to death? It defied all logic. They picked him up and carried him to the *Raven*.

AUTHOR'S NOTE

The seal fishery has historically been an important part of the economic structure of Newfoundland. The cost, however, has been extremely high in terms of the enormous loss of men and ships while *out to the ice*. While sealers were plying their trade on the vast ice-fields off Newfoundland's north coast and in the Gulf of St. Lawrence, there were always loved ones waiting at home for their safe return, fully aware of the extreme risks their men-folk were taking. "Pius Carroll Goes Swiling" is a fictional story about an eager and daring young man and his worried mother. Information for this story was based on *The Dictionary of Newfoundland English*, edited by G. M. Story, W. J. Kirwin, and J. D. A. Widdowson (Toronto: University of Toronto Press, 1982).

HOME FROM
THE WAR

*I*n the fall of 1915, three young men left their tiny settlement in Notre Dame Bay on the north coast of Newfoundland and made their way to the interior town of Grand Falls. There they caught the train to take them to the capital city of St. John's. This 330-mile trip was just the start of a longer and more terrible journey than they ever could have anticipated, a journey that would mark each of them forever and change them in ways they would never have imagined. They had left home united in a common purpose – to enlist in the First New-foundland Regiment and to go off to war to fight for their country.

The morning of July 1, 1916, eight months later, saw them, along with 798 other Newfoundland soldiers, awaiting the order to rise from their trenches and advance to engage the enemy at close quarters.

Five months after that, the same three young men, none yet having seen his twentieth birthday, were welcomed back home by the people of their small village. The people rejoiced in the fact that the three had survived the Battle of the Somme while so many of their comrades had perished under the withering machine-gun fire they had faced that fateful day. Their homecoming was a cause for great celebration, for only 69 of the 801 soldiers who had attempted to cross the no-man's land that separated them from the Germans had been left unscathed. All the others had been either killed or wounded.

The three young men who came back to this village, however, were not quite the same boys who had left. They were aged beyond their years and damaged beyond repair. They were nothing like the lads the community had previously known, and were clearly incapable of ever returning to the lives they had known before the war. Nevertheless, in the outport way, they would, despite their infirmities, be embraced in a communal blanket of love and support for as long as they might live. In the eyes of some, however, they would always remain objects of pity and compassion.

Elijah was the oldest. He had been eighteen when he enlisted. John and Cecil, both seventeen at the time, had lied convincingly enough to the recruitment officer to get themselves enlisted as well. Elijah was the first to come back home. He arrived two weeks before the others.

Elijah had not been wounded in the fighting in France, at least not physically. No lasting scar of any type marred his body, and, from that perspective, he was as healthy and as robust as he had been on the day he left. But for him, the big guns of the Somme still thundered in his ears and the carnage of Beaumont Hamel was still vivid in his mind. He simply could not forget and could not find the daily rhythm needed to get on with the rest of his life. He was trapped in a cycle of continuing horror from which he could not escape.

He walked. From morning to night, day after day, that was all he did. At first the people of the community were puzzled by the sight of this young man tramping for endless hours around the settlement and the surrounding countryside, seemingly lost within himself. But they soon grasped the undeniable reality that, as Uncle Ezra Porter put it, Elijah was shell-shocked. That realization, however, did not distract from their affection and respect for the young man, for had not the boy been prepared to make the supreme sacrifice on their behalf, to ensure their freedom and their way of life? To them, no matter what his condition, he was a war hero, and he was now theirs to look after and care for as best they could.

Elijah did not usually awake to begin his long periods of walking until late in the morning, quite often noon or even later. It was not laziness, but simply the heavy artillery and the blood and gore that would not permit him to sleep, and invariably, night after night, slumber would not come until daybreak. Then, sleep was fitful, and he generally awoke drained and almost too tired to face another day.

He walked for three years. Then his plight worsened when his mother, with whom he had lived since returning home, died. Oddly, it was this sad occurrence that set in motion the curious sequence of events that would finally set Elijah on the road to restoration and the achievement of a degree of happiness that had hitherto seemed impossible. A family relative, while searching through the drawers of a dresser looking for a suitable garment in which to bury his mother, had unearthed a dilapidated old fiddle and presented it to Elijah. The sight of the battered instrument stirred long-buried images in his mind. When he handled the fiddle, it felt comfortable and familiar in his hands.

Suddenly, despite the loss of his mother, a sense of purpose crept back into Elijah's life. He started working on the fiddle, trying to restore it to some semblance of working order. For hours on end he cleaned, rubbed, and polished until he was finally satisfied with its appearance. Then he set about trying to tune it. Vague memories of his father showing him how to do this as a young boy and teaching him how to play simple ditties strengthened in his mind as he worked. He tweaked and manipulated the fiddle's tuning pegs, and gradually the sound he was searching for emerged from the old instrument. In the process, the musical talent long dormant bubbled to the surface.

"Elijah's got his father's ear, that's for sure," Uncle Ezra would often say. "And there was never anyone better."

During the ensuing weeks and months, Elijah practised and experimented, mastering every song he put his mind to, until eventually, he had a repertoire of jigs, reels, hymns, and ballads, along with a number of his own compositions, to make any musician proud. When he played, he was as one with the fiddle. He would close his eyes and breathe deeply as he lived the music and the moment with every fibre of his being.

His walks became shorter and fewer.

And then he started something completely out of character. He began to appear at houses around the settlement, bringing his fiddle with him and playing his music for the people who lived there. His first appearances were tentative, and the recipients of his visits were surprised, if not shocked, to see him. But when he began to play, they knew they were being treated to something special, something wonderful which was being offered to them by this war-weary young man.

He developed a routine from which he rarely varied. He would show up in the evening, usually after supper dishes had been cleaned and put away. He did not want to impose himself on anyone for a meal; he simply came to play. He rarely spoke other than to say hello. Placing his scruffy green felt hat on the chair and sitting on it, he would make a few tentative strokes of his bow across the strings to make sure the instrument was in tune, and then launch into an hour's worth of playing. His impromptu kitchen concerts, given once a week, were never identical although the format was consistent. He would usually begin with a familiar hymn or two, or a ballad, followed by a long interlocking sequence of jigs and reels in which the transition from one song to the next was so masterful and transparent that everything blended wonderfully into a single uninterrupted medley. Then, the fiddle would become a violin and his last two or three offerings would be plaintive and haunting, and so poignant they invariably brought tears to the eyes of his listeners. Finally, standing and beating his rumpled hat back into shape, he would take his leave. Sometimes, he would accept the cup of tea and the biscuit or two he was usually offered before he left.

Elijah played his music for the people of his community once a week, month after month, for forty-two years. Over a period of several months he would visit every house in the settlement and would then start over again. He was never rejected. People welcomed him into their homes and were never disappointed. His playing brought a measure of joy into their lives, and his appearance was a welcome break from their lives of toil and hardship. For a few minutes every now and then they were able to forget their own troubles and simply enjoy themselves. Sometimes they sang along to Elijah's music as he played, or danced with each other around their hot kitchens. Even Aunt Sue, who was stone deaf, somehow felt the rhythm of his playing and tapped her feet to the beat of it. Sometimes they cried. And equally important, by his simple act of love and giving, Elijah himself was again made whole.

Elijah wasn't the only one who had difficulty adjusting to life after the war. John was having a great deal of trouble as well. His sufferings, though, unlike Elijah's, were readily apparent to everyone the moment he arrived back home. People who had known him all his life now had difficulty reconciling themselves to the fact that the walking skeleton they saw was the same brawny young man who had left them fifteen months earlier. His torment and despair were evident in his vacant stare and gaunt appearance. Their greatest shock, however, came from their discovery that he had come home without one of his limbs. His left leg was missing.

John retired to his parents' house and to the tiny bedroom at the top of the stairs that had always been his. For several months, he spent most of his waking hours there, reluctantly emerging only to take the meals his mother cajoled him into eating. No amount of coaxing on the part of his parents and others, however, could entice him from his sanctuary for anything else. In his depression, he had become a recluse.

Like Elijah, the horrific sounds and scenes of the battlefield still haunted him. He had by then, though, been able to compartmentalize them and they no longer overwhelmed him as they did his comrade. The root cause of his continuing despair was the loss of his leg, and that alone. He felt that he was no longer whole. He was incomplete, and the thought of people looking upon him and pitying him, undoubtedly referring to him as "poor John," was more than he could bear. Shame and humiliation dominated the gamut of emotions that coursed through him. At one point, in his frustration, he took his artificial leg down to the kitchen and dumped it into the wood-box and told his mother to burn it. He would get by on a crutch.

The anguish he had felt on that dreadful morning after the Battle of the Somme, when the field doctor told him that his leg would have to be amputated lest he die of gangrene poisoning, was infinitely worse than anything he had seen or experienced on the battlefield. Even the passage of time and his long convalescence in the hospital in England did little to ease his torment. He hadn't wanted to go home. He didn't want to live.

His state of depression continued with no end in sight. Luckily, as had been the case with Elijah, a small miracle occurred and John was finally able to begin the long climb out of his despair. John awoke earlier than usual one morning to sunbeams playing on his face. He arose, dressed himself, and went to the window to look out upon the new day, something he rarely did anymore. The early morning glint of sunlight on the calm harbour water gave it an extraordinarily blue hue, and the screeching of gulls and a loon's mournful call from somewhere in the harbour pleased his ear. Even the discordant barking of a dog couldn't distract him from the beauty in that moment. His eyes strayed to the land-wash directly below his window, and he watched the small coastal birds that frequented the beach pick at the kelp and seaweed that had been left exposed by the low tide. Occasionally, preying gulls swooped down at them, and they were forced to dart away or be devoured. Invariably, undeterred from their purpose, they returned mere seconds later. The warrior in John recognized the tenacity of these tiny creatures, and he suddenly felt different than he had in a long, long time.

He remained at the window, drinking in the scene as if seeing it for the first time, until his mother tapped on his door to tell him that his breakfast was ready. In that brief space of time he had come to the decision that he was finally ready to get on with the rest of his life, come what may. Furthermore, he was going to work. He was going to be a fisherman. He went down to the kitchen and retrieved his artificial leg from the wood-box and strapped it on. For the first time, the sight of it did not revolt him or cause him pain.

He told nobody about his plans, but when he finally came out of his room and ventured out into the settlement, his parents, friends, and relatives rejoiced in the fact that he was at last on the road to recovery. Over the next two weeks he acquired a small boat and enough fishing gear to make a start, and when he had done so, he rowed out through the narrows one misty morning to the fishing grounds that lay beyond, telling no one where he was going. He stayed out there all that day, and when he returned, fifteen codfish lay on the floorboards of his boat. Not much of a yield for a full day's work, but it was a start. Spent and sore from rowing after his long period of inactivity, he was satisfied that things would get better.

The ensuing weeks saw him on the fishing grounds every morning except Sunday, holding his own and gradually regaining the strength and stamina that had slipped away. Foul weather did not deter him. He watched what the other fishermen of the settlement did and if any of them ventured out in less than ideal conditions, he did too, and in that way learned how to gauge the weather and the tides for himself and to make his own decisions.

Everything went smoothly until he got caught in an unexpected summer squall and was forced to make a dash for shore. The moment the tempest erupted he grasped the gravity of his situation and immediately began to row toward the nearest point of land, his jib sail being of no use to him because the wind was blowing offshore directly toward him. The fury of the sudden storm intensified as he rowed, and he made little or no headway against the force of the wind. He feared being capsized or blown out to sea. He strove doggedly on until he was on the verge of utter collapse, and then he felt the miraculous crunch of gravel beneath the keel of his boat. He had come ashore almost three miles south of his intended port and had to wait there until the squall abated and he recovered enough strength to row home.

He was shaken by the experience, and for the first time was forced to acknowledge his vulnerability out there alone on the open water. While he was quite capable of rowing out to the fishing grounds and back home again in normal weather conditions, or even rough water, he realized that his one leg was not enough to enable him to balance his body properly for the extra leverage and power that was needed to see him safely home in conditions similar to what he had just experienced. He concluded that he needed a partner.

As he pondered the idea, he thought that it might also be nice to have someone in the boat with whom he could share the long lonely hours – someone he could tolerate for long periods of time and who could put up with him in return. He knew who he wanted, one of his old war buddies.

Cecil was his man. Even though he and Cecil hadn't seen much of each other since returning home, he knew enough from their war experiences to assure himself that Cecil was someone he could rely on and trust in any situation.

When he broached the matter with him, however, Cecil laughed and thought he was joking. "It must be bad enough with one cripple in the boat," he scoffed. "Why would you want another?"

Cecil's story was similar to John's. He, too, had come home an amputee, without his right leg. He also had the additional misfortune of losing his right arm in the war as well. Like John, he had become depressed and had withdrawn from all aspects of life in the community.

"I don't care, you're coming out with me tomorrow," John persisted, and Cecil, despite his protestations, found himself perched on the front thwart of the boat the next morning, propelled there by the sheer force of John's will. Cecil, there against his wishes, refused to participate in that day's fishing in any way and did not speak even once during the entire time. He wanted to put a firm end to the whole business before it advanced much further. John, however, was at his door again early the following morning and the scene of the previous day was replayed in its entirety: John insisting and Cecil resisting. In the end, however, Cecil found himself once again in John's boat. When John returned the third morning, he found Cecil waiting outside for him, sitting on his wooden lunch bucket with a set of oilskins slung across his shoulder.

Thus was born a partnership that would last for almost forty years. The people of the settlement would never cease to marvel at the sight of these two men, an amputee and a double amputee, clumping their way to their boat in the early morning hours and returning several hours later to clean and store their catch before once again clumping back to their homes for the night. Together, with only two legs and three arms between them, they braved the cold sea every morning in all weathers, and managed a degree of success. Cecil built up enormous strength in his one arm and provided the power and leverage, as well as the companionship, that John had sought. The two were shining examples for others in the community, who, when faced with hardships and adversity of their own, had only to think of John and Cecil, and their own problems would often seem minuscule in comparison.

In 1968, fifty years after the Great War, the community decided that they wanted to honour their three war heroes while there was still time, for few veterans of World War I were still living. In other settlements all around Newfoundland soldiers had returned home after the war to try to resume their normal lives. Some came back so maimed and disfigured physically or emotionally they couldn't cope, and lived out their days in pain and misery. Others could never surmount the horrors they had known at Beaumont Hamel and were never again the same men they once were. Still others, however, were able, somehow, to put the war behind them and get on with their occupations and the raising of their families. Elijah, John, and Cecil could be counted in this group. In the fullness of time, these three young men, each in his own unique way, transcended their tragic circumstances and enriched their community and the lives of the people in it and touched the hearts and souls of generations.

It was a cold frosty evening in mid-February when John and Cecil, along with Elijah, all three of them now old and frail, sat in the front of the building that served as the settlement's meeting hall, feeling slightly ill at ease as they looked at the expectant faces staring back at them. The four generations comprising the settlement's population were present, and every person there, from the oldest to the very youngest, knew the stories of the men they were paying homage to; love and respect for the three heroes were evident in the faces of everyone in attendance.

Elijah took the proceedings in stride, as did John and Cecil. The thunder still sometimes roared in his head, but it no longer overwhelmed him and he was able to push it aside and focus on other aspects of living. John's missing leg still ached as if it were there and he was often known to say, "I allow I'm the only man in the world that ever had arthritis in a wooden leg." Cecil, too, at times felt aches and pains in limbs that no longer existed.

The indomitable spirit that had guided their footsteps that morning in 1915 when they set off to war still breathed in each of them as strongly as ever. Individually they had been, and still were, inspirational models of courage and perseverance. Together they soared. And their community knew it.

AUTHOR'S NOTE

This fictional account of Elijah, John, and Cecil was inspired during a visit my wife and I made to a small community in Notre Dame Bay where we were invited into the home of a gentleman resident. While there, we were shown an artificial leg, proudly preserved as a family treasure, which had been worn by the man's father who had served in World War I, and we were told the war veteran's story.

Having lost a leg and having suffered other serious injuries during the Battle of the Somme, the soldier had eventually returned home, overcome his tragic circumstances, married and raised a large family, and lived out a productive life as a fisherman and respected member of his community.

Upon reflection, both my wife and I realized that this soldier's story was similar to those repeated in communities all over Newfoundland, for of the 801 soldiers who fought in the Battle of the Somme only 69 had been left physically unscathed. All of the others had either been wounded, many of them very seriously, or killed in action on the battlefield.

THE LIGHT IN
THE GARDEN

*E*ven though it wasn't Sunday and he wasn't supposed to be there, Ned was curled up on the settee in the front parlour reading his dog-eared copy of Zane Grey's *Riders of the Purple Sage* for at least the fifth time. As a twelve-year-old, he had many chores he was expected to do each day. Having completed them for now, he had quietly crept into the room reserved for the Sabbath and other special occasions to pursue his favourite pastime, a rare opportunity during weekdays. He was starting chapter two when his mother, Ruth, called from the kitchen.

"Ned," she said, "I want you to take this drop of soup over to Aunt Alice for me."

"Oh, no," he groaned. If he had known that was coming he would have tried to be somewhere else, Zane Grey or not. He hated having to go over to that place. It was so gloomy and depressing that he always came back feeling gloomy and depressed himself.

"Make sure you walk around the long way," his mother added, "so you won't spill any of it climbing over the fences. And remember to bring back the pot."

It hadn't always been so solemn over at Aunt Alice and Uncle Simon's house. In fact, not long ago, Ned had loved going over there because it was so bright and cheerful. His aunt and uncle always made a fuss over him, and there was always a glass of syrup and a piece of cake or a few sweet biscuits to be had. To him it was like most other houses in the small community, a place where people laughed, carried on, and cared about each other. A place that made you feel welcome.

But no longer. He now went only when he was forced to – like now. Aunt Alice was sure to be there; she never left the house these days, but she was nothing like her old self. Usually when he went in now, Ned would find her crying and muttering about things that didn't make a whole lot of sense. Uncle Simon, on the other hand, was hardly ever home. He was usually up in the woods or roaming somewhere around the harbour. Ned had a feeling that Uncle Simon felt a lot like he did.

It had all started a little more than a year ago, around the middle of May, when Uncle Simon came over one morning to tell Jake, Ned's father, and Ruth about his experience the previous night.

"A funny thing happened," he told them. "I went out around the corner of the house to empty my bladder before I went to bed, like I always do, when I happened to glance up in the potato garden – and there was this light.

"It was the strangest thing," he continued. "It wasn't very big or very bright and it never moved around or flickered. I must have watched it for an hour or more and then it disappeared, just like that. I was watching it so long that Alice came out to see if anything was wrong with me, and she saw it too."

That was all. Jake and Ruth talked a little bit about it later, but neither of them really gave it much thought until Uncle Simon came back the next morning to repeat the same story – the light had been there again.

"Tell you what, Simon," Jake told him. "If you see it again tonight, let me know, and I'll come and have a look at it too."

Sure enough, that night, an hour or so after nightfall, Uncle Simon tapped on their door and poked his head in to tell them that the light was there again.

"Ned," Jake told his son, "stay here with your mother. I won't be gone long."

Ned protested, "I'm coming too."

Surprisingly, for once, Ruth came down on Ned's side. "I'm sure it will be all right, Jake. There's nothing to harm him."

Ned smiled to himself. Obviously, she wanted to go herself. His father wasn't pleased to be challenged, but after he and Ned's mother argued for a few minutes, they agreed that they would all go over to see what this light was all about.

And there it was, just as Uncle Simon said. It was hard to say for sure how close it was or how far away. It could have been just a few feet or it could have been all the way up to the top of the garden, perhaps even farther – there was just no way of telling. Ned and his parents watched it until it disappeared, just like Uncle Simon said it had the night before. They waited a little while longer to see if it would reappear. When it didn't, they all went home. When he was upstairs in bed later that night, Ned could still hear his mother and father talking about it down in the kitchen. He felt oddly disconcerted.

The light was there again the next night and the night after that. By that time Aunt Alice was convinced that it was a token.

"It's Harold, I'm sure of it," she insisted. "There's something wrong and he's trying to let us know."

Harold was their only son. Uncle Simon and Aunt Alice had three other children, all daughters, but they were all married and had by then moved out on their own. Harold and a boy named Tom Peddle from across the harbour, along with two other young men from the other side of the bay, had all left together several months earlier to go to St. John's to sign up for the war. Aunt Alice and Uncle Simon hadn't heard anything about Harold for a long while until one day they received a letter from him letting them know that he was over in France. The envelope also contained money from his soldier's pay. Aunt Alice never spent it. She just put it away in her bureau to give back to him when he came home again after the war.

Night after night for a full week the light reappeared for an hour or so, and then disappeared, just like clockwork. The two families looked for it every night. After a while they began to wish that it would just go away. It was starting to play on their nerves. Sometimes Ned got the cold shivers and felt the hairs rising on the back of his neck when he saw it, and instinctively stayed as close as possible to his parents' sides. When he went to bed afterwards, he sometimes asked his father to stay with him until he went to sleep.

By that time Aunt Alice had herself worked into a state of anxiety. She was sure Harold was dead, that that was what the light was trying to tell them. She cried and moaned for hours on end and nothing Ned's mother and father, Uncle Simon, or anyone else could say to her could comfort her or get her to stop. It finally got so bad that Ned's father said he was going to do something about it.

"I'm going to go up there the next time to see for myself what that light really is," he vowed. "This has gone on long enough."

Ned's mother didn't want him to go.

"I don't care," he insisted. "I can't stand this every night. And if someone doesn't do something about it, Alice will soon be off her head."

So the next night, while the rest of them waited, Ned's father went up in the darkness, crawling on his hands and knees most of the way. Even though the others couldn't see him, they could hear him grunting and panting as he made his way over the hard ground. They were all on pins and needles. The minutes seemed like hours. Then suddenly they heard a loud guffaw and then Jake clumping his way back, laughing as he came.

"Here's your token, Alice," he said, and passed her a piece of broken glass. "Every night," he explained, "when the moon is in a certain position in the sky, its light reflects off that piece of glass, which just happens to be in such a position that it can only be seen from your house and nowhere else.

"Then," he continued, "when the moon moves farther along in the sky and gets too far out of position to reflect on the glass anymore, the light just disappears. It's as simple as that."

That made a lot of sense, or so it seemed to Ned, because they could never see it from their own house even though it was only a short distance away.

"Thank God!" said Aunt Alice, "I'm some glad that's over. I was some worried."

After that they forgot all about it. Then, a few weeks later, the mail came and Silas Spurrell, the man who operated the mail-ferry, came directly over to Uncle Simon and Aunt Alice's house with a letter. Aunt Alice knew what it was even before she opened it because of the black border around the envelope. The letter was from the War Office, notifying her that Harold had been killed in action and was now buried in a small village in France with a number of other Newfoundland soldiers who had fallen in battle with him.

The news of Harold's death shocked them all, especially Aunt Alice. She was devastated. She withdrew into herself and resisted all efforts to be comforted or consoled. Before this tragedy she had always visited the home of Ruth and Jake at least once a day, usually on the pretext of borrowing or returning something but really with the intention of having a cup of tea and a chat. Now she never left her own house. Concerned, Ruth dropped over to see her every now and then, but all Aunt Alice did was rock in her chair and cry, and Ruth could rarely get a sensible word out of her.

A day or so after they'd learned of Harold's death, Ruth, Jake, and Ned were sitting around the supper table when Ruth suddenly stopped what she was saying in mid-sentence.

"What date was Harold killed?" she asked.

"July first," Jake replied. "I think that's what it said in the letter."

"That's what I thought," Ruth said. "You know," she continued after a slight pause, "I believe that was the first night the light appeared up in Simon's potato garden, wasn't it? Oh well, just a coincidence, I suppose."

They had all nodded uneasily.

Now, even though the light and Harold's death had occurred a year earlier, it seemed to Ned that they had happened only yesterday.

After he delivered the soup and returned to pick up where he'd left off in *Riders of the Purple Sage*, he felt strangely out of sorts. A sense of loneliness and uneasiness gripped him.

"How is Aunt Alice today?" his mother asked.

"All right, I suppose," Ned answered. "She's over there now, knitting socks and cuffs for Harold. She says he'll need them, with the cold weather coming on, because those he took with him must be full of holes by now."

"The poor old soul," his mother murmured. "And did you remember to bring back my pot?"

AUTHOR'S NOTE

In most communities throughout Newfoundland, superstition and belief in the supernatural have traditionally been part of the community fabric. Ghost stories from years gone by still abound and are still being told today. Many of them are horrible and chilling, yet are sworn to be the gospel truth. Tokens, in particular, played a significant part in people's lives. Often appearing in the form of mysterious and unexplained lights, these tokens were generally accepted as harbingers of death or catastrophe. The fictional story "The Light in the Garden" is rooted in this belief.

ON GANDER LAKE

*A*t six o'clock, sufficient light from the mid-March sun still filtered through the treetops to permit an unobstructed passage through the woods. The unseasonable warmth of the day showed no sign of abating, and the long shadows cast by the radiant western horizon lent a surreal touch of serenity to the waning afternoon hours. The boughs of the spruce, pine, and fir trees dripped the last remnants of the ice and snow that had encased them only that very morning, and tiny rivulets of water, freed after months of icy confinement, cut trenches in every direction. The gentle breeze that drifted softly from the southwest held the promise of even better things to come. Yet, despite the beauty of the moment, the surrounding countryside still lay dormant under a blanket of white as far as the eye could see, and Gander Lake remained frozen along its entire length and breadth, and would not thaw for weeks to come.

A heavily laden figure emerged from the forest and paused at the edge of the woods. He cautiously surveyed his surroundings, a habit bred from a lifetime of wilderness living. The monster of a black dog at his side did likewise, sniffing the air in every direction. Satisfied by what he saw, the man covered the short distance to the beach and propped his long-gun up against one of the boulders that lined the shore of the lake. He removed his snowshoes, traps, and backpack and deposited them on the ground. Rapping the snowshoes sharply against each other to dislodge the bits of ice and snow that clogged the frames and the rawhide webbing, he resisted the urge to hurl them into the distance. The trek through the woods had not been easy. The early morning hours had been relatively trouble-free and he had made good progress. The rising temperature and softening snow, however, had gradually rendered the snowshoes useless until he eventually abandoned them entirely, preferring to sink to his knees with virtually every step rather than put up with the frustration of having to stop every few yards to clean away the layers of sticky mush that accumulated and stuck to them like glue. At one point he had considered jettisoning the load he was carrying on his back and returning later to retrieve it, but then decided against it, opting instead to try to ignore the irritation and proceed doggedly onward as best he could.

The burly frame and brute strength of the man were evident even under the large, filthy fur coat he wore, and his fluid movements bespoke a creature acutely attuned to the environment in which he existed. With his coat and cap now removed, the sweat of his exertion dampened his dirty woollen undershirt, and plastered his black oily hair to the sides of his head. Dripping, stinging water forced him to wipe his brow and eyes every few minutes. He intended to take just a short spell before continuing onward to his cabin a half mile away on the northwestern corner of the lake.

The dog, vigilant while relaxing, bore an uncanny resemblance to its master. Even in repose, its sheer size and the muscles that rippled under its fur were evidence of its primeval strength and power. Its yellow eyes suggested more than a hint of wolf in its bloodline and gave it an aura that bordered on menacing. Rough and filthy like its master who had found it and reared it from a pup, the animal brooded with a sinister presence. It was a beast no man would ever wish to encounter if alone and unarmed. The dog was now oblivious to the oozing wounds suffered on its shoulder and flank a day or two earlier. Its licking had already congealed the affected areas somewhat and stemmed the flow of blood, and that was good enough for now. Time would do the rest.

The man was tired, bone weary from twelve hours of hard slogging. The wet clothes that clung to his sweat-covered body had already begun to chill, despite the warm weather. Although he had eaten that morning, he was now ravenous again. More than anything else, he wanted his pipe, to experience the soothing pleasantness of the smoke as it filled his lungs. For a brief moment, he was tempted to spread his coat out on the frozen ground and lie down on it, and just let himself drift off as he had sometimes done in the past. The last time he had done that, though, he had awakened shivering violently and had been forced to spend the next three days on the broad of his back in his cabin while chills and fevers alternately racked his body. He had vowed that he would never do that again.

In the end, it was his craving for tobacco that prompted him to go on. He had smoked the last of his that morning. Before leaving to run his trap-line three days earlier, he had carefully rationed out the amount he estimated he would need while he was away, and had spared it along with great prudence and self-discipline, denying the urge to light up until he could stand it no longer. But now his tobacco pouch was empty. Just a short distance away lay the last of the hoard he had purchased in Twillingate the previous fall. It was hidden securely under the floorboards of his cabin, safe from any prowler who might happen by. He knew that the first thing he would do when he got home was to light up and have a good smoke.

The circuit of his trap-line, totalling more than ten miles in distance, had been rewarding, much better than he had expected. The weather had been good and the sleek pelts of the pine marten, foxes, muskrats, and otters he had found in his snares and metal traps were of prime quality. They would undoubtedly fetch top dollar when he brought them to Twillingate in May. In the meantime he would leave them safely cached along his trap-line until it was time to retrieve them for market.

During the three-day trek, he and the dog had gorged themselves on the rich dark meat of the skinned carcasses until they were both sated, unable to cram in another mouthful. Afterward, they rested blissfully for a few hours until their bloated and lethargic bodies summoned up enough energy to carry on again.

The only sore point of the trip had been the fact that he had found six of his metal traps in disrepair. The jaws of two of them were rusted together so badly he could not pry them open, even using the barrel of his long-gun as a lever, so he discarded them on the spot. The other four he deemed salvageable. An application of animal fat and oil, along with some elbow grease, would restore their usefulness, and he decided to bring these traps home with him. His traps, some of which were of ancient vintage, were his means of livelihood and he intended to extract the maximum use from them.

Reshouldering his backpack, snowshoes, and traps, he resumed his homeward journey, knowing he would now have to cover the remaining distance in the rapidly gathering darkness. His route lay across the northwestern corner of the lake, a path he had trodden so many times since the lake had frozen over last fall that his footprints forged a line in the ice straight to his cabin door. To follow the shoreline would entail twice the distance, and in the soft snow, would take him that much longer. In any case, the ice of the lake was still firm enough to bear his considerable weight, and would remain so well into April.

The dog, as anxious as its master to reach the comforts of the cabin, paced, never far from the man's side. No overt communication of any kind passed between them, yet the bond and understanding between man and beast were unmistakable. They were partners, relying on each other for companionship and protection.

Halfway to his destination, the man stopped to rest again for a few minutes. His legs were beginning to cramp from the long hours of hard walking, and he stooped slightly to rub them to restore circulation. This time he did not bother to remove the load from his back. He wasn't planning to stop very long.

The loud low explosions that frequently reverberated across the ice caused him no concern. Neither did the long jagged crack lines that marked the ice surface in numerous places. They simply spelled the beginning of spring thaw as the many layers of ice that covered the lake to a depth of several feet in some areas grounded and grated against each other below the frigid surface. The first real indication that the ice was becoming unsafe would be the appearance of open pools of water along the shoreline. None of these were yet visible. The other potential peril, soft areas caused by shifting undercurrents, underground springs, and warm spots in the lake's depths, were usually identifiable by a discolouring of the ice in those particular areas. The man had not noted any of these yet this year.

The discomfort of his legs assuaged somewhat, he started out again. By now, night had descended in full, and the darkness rendered his progress a little more difficult, although he knew his way across the frozen lake by heart. The dog, meandering ahead, knew instinctively that he was now charged with some of the responsibility for getting his master and himself safely home.

The man had advanced no more than a dozen paces when he heard the dog growl, and knew instantly that something was amiss. When the growls became whines and sharp yips, he immediately turned back, implicitly placing his trust in the animal's instincts. Clearly, some danger lay ahead. He would have to retrace his steps and approach the cabin from a different direction.

But it was too late. He felt the ice open beneath him, and even as he tried to straddle the danger area, he felt himself falling. Suddenly up to his waist in the shockingly frigid water, he clung to the edge of the ice, trying frantically to pull himself up. He hung there for several seconds, and then, to his disbelief, the ice failed under his weight and he plunged below the surface. He struggled upward but the load on his back kept pulling him down. He knew that his only chance of survival was to remove it. He desperately tried to dislodge the traps securely tied across his shoulders.

To his horror, the rope was snagged, and the backpack, metal   69
traps, and snowshoes were all entangled with each other. He tried to
shuck out of his fur coat, but the same rope bound it too tightly.
He was trapped and running out of time. His lungs were bursting
and he was forced to exhale, spitting a stream of bubbles to the
surface. Still, he refused to inhale, but finally, the searing in his chest
forced him to gasp – he had to breathe, he had to have air. Instead, icy
water rushed in and filled his mouth, and then his lungs. His frantic
struggles slowed until they finally ceased altogether and the panic
magically transformed itself into calm acceptance. Limp, his body
drifted to the bottom of the lake.

The dog howled into the night, its grief echoing across the lake
into the darkness. It held a lonely vigil. When it was finally over, he
set off, not toward the cabin, but back across the lake toward the
dark woods that lay beyond, leaving behind him forever the only
companion he had ever known.

AUTHOR'S NOTE

Who was this man who met such an untimely death on Gander Lake? His name was Noel Boss, and history records that
he was a furrier who trapped and traded furs in the Notre
Dame Bay area of Newfoundland's northeast coast in the early
to mid 1800s. It is known that he was of Mi'kmaq descent and
that he was well known to many of the European settlers living
in that area, and had, in fact, on a number of occasions visited
the home of John Peyton, Jr., a renowned merchant in Exploits
who later became the magistrate of Twillingate.

It is clear that Boss was a competent and experienced woodsman, and was in that respect not unlike many other furriers

who operated in the area at that time. But there the similarities end. For he was something else – something far more sinister. He was reputedly a hunter of humans, a predator who stalked and ambushed men, women, and children and killed them indiscriminately. He was arguably one of the worst murderers that Newfoundland has ever known. He not only killed people, he kept count and openly boasted about his foul deeds. At the time of his drowning, his tally stood at ninety-nine, and his stated objective was to "kill an even hundred" before he was through.

Unbelievably, this man was never charged or prosecuted for his crimes even though they were well known and he himself made no effort to conceal them. For his victims were not white settlers. They were Beothuk Indians. Although laws had been enacted by the early 1800s to prevent the persecution of the Beothuk, they were rarely enforced, and the killing of natives, which had started not long after John Cabot made his landfall at Bonavista in 1497, continued unchecked.

One of his intended victims was Shanawdithit, the young woman believed to have been the last of the Beothuk race. In her captivity, she related how she had been cleaning venison by the side of a brook one day when she looked up and saw him aiming his long gun at her from the opposite side. She fled and escaped, but not before receiving shotgun wounds to her arm, hand, and foot. Although she survived her injuries, she walked with a limp for the rest of her life. The fact that Boss himself escaped death until he met his demise by his own traps on Gander Lake attests to the man's cunning and woodsmanship, for undoubtedly he was well known to the Beothuk and would have been one of their prime targets.

If viewed from the perspective of the size of the entire Beothuk population, which some historians suggest never exceeded more than a thousand, the contribution of Noel Boss and a few others of his ilk to the eventual extinction of the Beothuk people is nothing short of staggering.

Two hundred years or more have elapsed since the incident on Gander Lake, and the shameful eradication of the Beothuk race is now a distant part of our history. Our museums offer displays of Beothuk artifacts, and at Boyd's Cove in Notre Dame Bay an actual Beothuk encampment site has been discovered and preserved. Some knowledge of the language and culture of the Beothuk race has been handed down to us by Shanawdithit and her aunt, Demasduit (Mary March), during their brief stays in captivity. And somewhere in the murky depths of Gander Lake lie the bones of a murderous villain of the worst order.

This depiction of Noel Boss is based primarily on information contained in Joseph R. Smallwood's *Encyclopedia of Newfoundland and Labrador* (St. John's: Newfoundland Book Publishers Limited, 1967, 1981) and *The Book of Newfoundland* (St. John's: Newfoundland Book Publishers Limited, 1967). Some other publications, such as Michael Crummey's *River Thieves* (Toronto: Doubleday Canada, 2001) and James P. Howley's *The Beothucks or Red Indians* (Cambridge: Cambridge University Press, 1915), portray him in a kinder light, emphasizing the colourful nature of his character and his prowess as a hunter and woodsman, while downplaying any predatory tendencies he may have had toward the Beothuk.

THE SKRAELING[5]

*R*alf drained his tankard and wiped his beard with his sleeve. He leaned forward and the din of the longhouse subsided. He waited until he had their undivided attention. They watched him expectantly, listening intently. For most of them, it had been a long dreary winter, and they were restless and eager for action. The inactivity and tedium of the frozen months had rendered them lethargic, and they needed something to snap them out of their state of boredom. This could be the moment.

Massive, with long red hair and matching beard, piercing blue eyes, and a perpetual scowl, Ralf was the undisputed leader of this small cluster of humanity perched precariously on the northernmost tip of the large island now known as Newfoundland, two thousand miles from the homeland they had left four years earlier. Outside, ice pellets battered the longhouse, but in the sweltering dimness of its crowded interior, sweat glinted on Ralf's high forehead and flickering light from the oil lantern projected and distorted his shadow on the peat wall behind him.

Kjersti was as anxious as the others to hear what her husband would say. Swollen in her seventh month of pregnancy, she knew that her condition would have little or no bearing on his decision, yet hoped, futilely perhaps, that he would at least take it into consideration. If he and

---

[5] Skraeling is the ancient Norse term for the aboriginal people (Dorset) of Greenland with whom the Vikings would have undoubtedly come in contact. During their stay in Newfoundland, the Vikings applied this same term to the aboriginal people they found to be living there, most likely the Beothuk or their predecessors.

the others went away now, they might be gone for a long time, perhaps months or even longer, and she wanted him to be here with her when their child was born. Woman's foolishness, she conceded, but such were her thoughts nevertheless. Perhaps he would wait a while, just a few more weeks.

Her wish was not to be.

"It's time," Ralf told them. Anticipation rippled through the room. "We leave in a fortnight," he continued, "as soon as we can get the knarr ready."

The voyage had been talked about for months, although many of the details entailed in such a venture had scarcely been mentioned. Ralf would articulate these in due course, and the others were just as happy to leave them to him. All that was important to them was the date of their departure and their destination. They were rovers, and the sedentary existence of the past three years had made them uneasy. Weeks of debate had centred on which direction they would take, with some favouring going south along the east coast of the strange new land, while others promoted the idea of sailing westward again. Their purpose was to seek a suitable location for a second settlement or the relocation of their present site, somewhere a little warmer and a little more forgiving than here, where the winter winds blew incessantly and fog sometimes shrouded the land for weeks on end.

"We'll take a crew of seven, including myself," Ralf told them. "Gunnar and Kjell, of course, and Kai. Ambjorg, too, and two others. Bjoern and Andor, I think they'd be best. The rest of you will be needed here.

"In case the skraelings come," he added.

Both elation and disappointment filled the longhouse. Every man there wanted desperately to be included in the venture, yet knew full well that they all couldn't go. Ralf had spoken, and argue as they might, those not named knew there was little likelihood of getting him to change his mind.

One person in particular felt the disappointment more keenly than anyone else. Despite being rebuffed on a number of previous requests, Peder still held the hope of being among the chosen few who would go when the time came.

"I want to come, too," he pleaded. "I can do a man's work, and I'm not really needed here all that much."

"Peder, Peder, what am I to do with you?" Ralf's strong hands gripped the boy's shoulders. "Three times you've asked me, and three times I've told you no. You're too young. Your turn will come, but not yet.

"Besides," he continued, "You're more important here than you think. I'll be counting on you while I'm away."

Ralf's words did little to diminish the boy's disappointment. Since the voyage of exploration had first arisen, Peder's thoughts had been dominated by the desire to be a part of it. Nothing else mattered. The prospect of venturing off where no one had ever gone before thrilled him, and his obsession had grown with each passing day. The boy's dream was now crushed.

The ensuing days, charged with renewed energy and sense of purpose, saw the knarr's canvas unrolled and spread out upon the ground to be scrutinized for defects. The vessel's riggings were inspected, repaired, and replaced where necessary, and boiled pitch was applied to its hull. Innumerable other repairs, both small and major, were performed under the careful eye of Kjell, the carpenter, to make the knarr ready for the voyage ahead. Two years of being beached and neglected had taken its toll, and much work was needed to restore the vessel to its previous seaworthy condition.

Finally, two days later than Ralf had hoped, the knarr was ready. The wind was right and the day fair. With supplies for an extended journey stored on board and the seven seafarers at their positions, the vessel, with its big black sail unfurled, slowly navigated the narrow channel toward the open sea, picking up speed as it moved away from the land. Those left behind watched. Some waved and cheered. Some, Kjersti among them, felt sadness. Ralf's child kicked inside her, within weeks, perhaps days, of being born.

Ralf and his crew sailed southward, skirting the shoreline, exploring the numerous bays and coves, noting specific areas of interest for further investigation on their homeward journey. They took on fresh water whenever they needed it from some of the great flowing rivers they happened upon. The fine weather held, although the nights were still very cold and the morning sun invariably took an hour or more to thaw the ice that had formed overnight on the knarr's riggings and gunwales.

On the second morning out of port, none other than Peder emerged from his hiding place among the knarr's cargo – a stowaway. His desire to be part of this expedition had overwhelmed his fear. He reasoned that Ralf would not turn back just to take him back home. They might put him ashore to make his own way home or, at worst, throw him overboard into the sea. He hoped they would let him continue on with them.

Now exposed, he waited for Ralf's reaction, his young body tense and defiant.

Ralf, as Peder had feared, exploded into violent rage. Only the gentle interjections of Kjell, the carpenter, saved the boy from a serious beating – or worse. The leader, thus checked, vented his great anger instead through an expletive-laced tirade against the youth, some of it directed at Kjell as well. The crew, having experienced Ralf's violent temper before, kept their distance and maintained their silence. Gradually, Ralf brought himself under control until eventually he seemed to find some humour in the situation. He threw his head back and laughed uproariously.

"Peder, you young devil," he said. "There's not much I can do about you now but make you work your fingers to the bone. 'Ere long you'll be begging me to take you home."

Thus, Peder found himself a member of the expedition, albeit of untenable standing. He vowed to himself that in the coming days he would make Ralf come to see him as a worthy addition to his crew.

The next two days went well from Peder's point of view, although he gave Ralf as wide a berth as the confines of the knarr would allow. Ralf himself seemed to have put the episode behind him. In fact, Ralf was beginning to feel apprehensive. He couldn't pinpoint the cause of his uneasiness. Perhaps it was the fact that they had completed several days of uneventful and leisurely exploration of the ragged coastline. Such a long period of tranquility was rare.

Late that afternoon Ralf decided to go ashore. The beach, at least half a mile long, with glistening sand and a rushing river flowing into the sea, beckoned him. It held interesting possibilities for the relocation of their present settlement. He decided they would spend the night there. He guided the knarr slowly toward the beach until its keel grated softly against the soft sand. Leaving only Bjoern on board, he and the others waded the final few feet to the shore.

No sooner had they reached the sand than a horde of screaming assailants descended upon them, brandishing fearsome weapons of all types.

"Skraelings!" yelled Ralf. "Go back, go back."

But it was too late. Their attackers were upon them instantly. Peder, the last one to leave the knarr, saw Kai pirouette and fall to the sand, multiple arrows protruding from his body. He watched as Gunnar fell under a torrent of axes. A little farther up the beach Ralf was trying vainly to fend off a pack of attackers, swinging wildly with his great fists even as his life's blood flowed from his body. To Peder it all seemed to be happening in slow motion, violent images frozen in time.

In just minutes they were all dead, their mutilated bodies strewn about the beach, their blood discolouring the sand and the waters of the nearby shoreline. Only Peder, and perhaps Bjoern on the knarr, remained alive.

Peder now awaited his certain doom.

Two men grabbed him and screamed at him. A third raised his ax to deliver the fatal blow. Despite his terror, Peder did not look away. His Viking soul compelled him to look into the eyes of his slayer even to the moment of death.

But the blow did not fall. A fourth attacker stayed the arm of Peder's would-be executioner. An argument ensued among the four. Loud guttural utterances and menacing gestures punctuated the discussion. At one point the fourth man grabbed Peder's long red hair and gestured violently.

Finally, the four reached some type of agreement, and Peder's life was spared. He was led away as a captive of the feared skraelings.

Days later he was led into the skraeling encampment where he was immediately surrounded, an object of great fascination. Hands poked and prodded him, examining him all over as the people tried to satisfy their curiosity about this strange young man with the white skin, blue eyes, and flaming red hair – attributes all in stark contrast to their own dark features. It was his hair that seemed to interest them the most, and they took turns running their hands through it, tugging at it, smelling it, and in some cases licking it to see if the colour was fast or perhaps applied like the red ochre that many of them wore on their own faces and bodies. Most of them were relatively gentle, although one or two attempted to manhandle him until they were deterred by a sharp reprimand from one of the elders, whom Peder assumed was the leader of the tribe. Children howled and hooted as they whirled and danced around him. One woman touched his face softly and Peder recognized a hint of compassion in her eyes. Although the skraelings had known of the existence of white warriors in the area to the north of them, this was the first time any of them had actually seen such a creature in the flesh. This one didn't seem as fearsome as they had envisaged. He was young, though, and perhaps not yet hardened into the brutal ways of adulthood.

His first few days in the encampment were a blur of misery and activity totally foreign to him. He was given over to the women, where he was expected to help with womanly work – cooking, curing animal hides, gathering fuel, cleaning, and a multitude of other tasks. For hours on end he was made to chew on caribou skins until they were soft and supple enough to satisfy the women. His teeth ached and bled, and the residue from the fresh hides stuck in his throat and kept him constantly nauseated.

His initial efforts were invariably met with laughter and hoots of derision. Gradually, though, as he learned to do the work better, and as the weeks passed, he was left increasingly alone. The novelty of his presence in the encampment was wearing off, and his days and nights no longer found him the object of ridicule.

Aside from a scattered slight cuffing or swipe with the hand, Peder was not seriously mistreated, and he somehow managed to get enough food to stay alive. He often felt cold and wet, for some days still brought bitterly cold temperatures and hard rains. Although he was grateful for being left in peace much of the time, he was often lonely and sad. At times, he even harboured a longing to talk with the people. Now accustomed to their ways and manner of living, he could see that they were not quite the savages he had always thought them to be.

The woman who had caressed his cheek the day he arrived came to see him now and again. She sometimes brought him a morsel of food, and on one occasion, a garment of caribou skin. When he shed his own tattered and threadbare clothing and put it on, the soft hide felt comfortable against his flesh. Her visits cheered him.

A boy not much older than himself also established a relationship of sorts with Peder. The skraeling youth had, at first, been hostile toward Peder and had threatened him with fierce scowls and menacing gestures. Peder stood his ground, however, and refused to flinch or give way to the threats, until finally the young skraeling turned abruptly on his heel and left. Successive appearances followed the same pattern, and, although the skraeling's visits were rooted in intimidation and belligerence, Peder began to look forward to them. A least they provided a departure from the monotony of his meagre existence.

Then one day Peder's adversary, having completed his usual charade, thumped his own chest with his fists and uttered the word "Asbut." He did it repeatedly, enunciating the word each time until Peder grasped the notion that the skraeling was telling him his name, whereupon he pounded his own chest and said, "Peder," repeatedly, until the skraeling nodded. Unable to understand another word of each other's languages, they now knew each other by name, and a fledging friendship began.

They spent time together nearly every day, sometimes just a few minutes, other times for hours at a time, talking to each other through gestures. One afternoon Asbut came and entered into a long and heated discussion with the women. He then took Peder by the arm and led him away.

Asbut led Peder through the woods to the nearby river whose roaring waters he had heard in the distance but never seen. There, Asbut pointed out the hundreds of salmon lining the bottom of a shallow pool, so densely packed they rested in layers above and below each other, pausing there before continuing their migration upstream to their spawning grounds. He positioned Peder next to the still waters of the pool, indicating that he was to stay there while he himself splashed about trying to drive the fish toward Peder. When Asbut used his hands to flip salmon from the water toward Peder, the young Viking readily understood that he was supposed to catch them, kill them, and place them on the grassy spot behind him.

An hour later they had landed a large number of the sleek silver fish which they then brought back to the encampment. Because of the salmon's great size, they could carry only two or three at a time.

The salmon remained in the pool for five more days before continuing their journey upstream. During that time Asbut and Peder landed many, many more, a valuable contribution to the overall welfare of the encampment. The salmon, when cured, smoked, and cached, would be a staple of their winter food supply.

The catching of the salmon also resulted in a big change for Peder. He was transferred from the supervision of the women into Asbut's mamateek, where he ate with Asbut and his family, slept with them, shared their work, learned some of their language, and in almost every respect functioned as a family member. He had been adopted.

He now lived in a man's world, no longer expected to do womanly tasks. He hunted with the men and went with them on their excursions. He wrestled with the other young men of the encampment and raced against them, often besting them at their own games. He had, in the space of a few short months, adapted to the skraeling way of life and found a degree of happiness and contentment he would never have thought possible when he was first captured.

But when he went to sleep at night he still dreamed the dreams of a Viking, of being in the longhouse with the mingled smells of sweat, ale, and peat, of listening to the ribaldry and laughter of Ralf and the others as they gathered at the end of the day to tell their stories. The face of his mother, Agata, the seamstress, still hovered over him as he slept. Despite his growing attachment to Asbut and the others, the thought of escaping was ever-present.

Autumn approached and the days grew shorter and colder. Then one day, Eduit, the chieftain, announced that it was time to begin preparations for the annual caribou hunt. Several days were spent organizing the event, until early one morning six canoes, each carrying four men, set out from the encampment and paddled northward – twenty-four hunters in all, Peder among them.

A full day of hard travel brought them to the deer fences. These were structures of rocks, sticks and fallen trees several miles long, toward which hunters would drive caribou from the migrating herds. Then they would try to turn them and force them to run alongside the fence until the fleeing animals were forced into narrow passes where other hunters were waiting to kill them with lances and arrows. This ancient device had been erected by Asbut's ancestors and had traditionally enabled his people to harvest large numbers of caribou. The annual caribou hunt was vital to the encampment's continued survival. The meat was the most essential part of their winter diet, and the hides and bones were essential for their clothing, tools, and shelter.

Peder, seeing the deer fences for the first time, could not visualize how the operation would unfold. Asbut had explained to him through gestures and drawings in the sand that they would be hunting caribou, but that was all he knew. He would simply have to stay alert, watch the others, and follow their lead.

Having beached their canoes, some of the group, including Peder, proceeded eastward until they were a considerable distance away from the fence. There they concealed themselves to wait until the caribou herd arrived. The others positioned themselves along the passes at the southern end of the fence, to wait there until the animals were driven toward them. The waiting period could be as short as a day or two or extend into weeks. Some years the caribou did not come at all. A failed hunt meant a winter of hardship and starvation.

On the fifth day the caribou came. The hunters waited in position until the major portion of the herd was between them and the fence. Then they emerged to race en masse toward the herd, screaming, striking their noise makers, and brandishing weapons to make themselves as terrifying as possible, striving to frighten the animals and force them toward the fence, and then turn them to the south where the other hunters waited. Peder followed in the rear, trying his best to emulate the others.

Pandemonium ensued – pounding hooves, snorting and bellowing animals, screaming men, dust, flying ground cover. Amid all the noise and confusion, Peder suddenly realized that this was his opportunity to escape – perhaps the only chance he might ever have. He was already several miles north of the encampment and, with a river to take him even farther north, he knew he could probably travel far before nightfall. That is, if the hunters didn't miss him. He was willing to gamble that they were all so intently focused on the hunt that his departure would go unnoticed.

He ran a short distance behind the others before veering off, running low, his heart beating wildly in his chest. He was committed now; there was no turning back. If he was seen now it would all be over.

When he reached the canoes he looked back over his shoulder and saw that no one was following him. Indeed, the distance between him and the others was widening rapidly as the hunters chased the caribou toward the passes. He pushed one of the canoes into the water. It was much heavier than he had expected and required considerable effort to move it. He paddled the craft into mid-stream where the water flowed faster, and took one last look back to make sure he hadn't been spotted. Then, paddling furiously and trying to keep the canoe straight, he let the river take him northward. Somewhere to the north were his own people, what was left of them, and he hoped that if he kept going north he would eventually find them.

He paddled all day until nightfall forced him to beach the canoe and go ashore. He made himself a bed of boughs and leaves. He was tired and cold, but sleep would not come, for his thoughts were racing with excitement and the worry that he must put as much distance between himself and the others as quickly as possible. He rested fitfully for several hours, listening to the night noises before he finally drifted off to sleep.

When he awoke in the morning, stiff and sore from his previous day's exertions, the sun was already high in the sky. Panic gripped him. He had overslept and lost much valuable time. He grabbed several handfuls of partridgeberries from along the riverbank and stuffed them into his mouth. It was the first food he had eaten in almost two full days. He pushed the canoe back into the water and braced himself for another day of hard paddling.

Peder spent that day and most of the next following the river, paddling and steering the canoe to avoid rocks and tree snags. Occasionally, to conserve his strength, he let the current carry him along while he rested. He went ashore a few times to search for berries or anything else he could find to eat. At one point, using his hands, he caught three small brook trout and ate them raw.

Early one morning he came to the falls. He'd heard the thunder and felt the quickening current long before he arrived. The falls were very high and steep, and Peder realized there was no way he could skirt them and continue his journey by canoe. From here on he would have to travel on foot.

He climbed a high ridge to try to get his bearings. Off to the east he saw the ocean, and instinctively understood that if he simply followed the coastline he must eventually reach the settlement of his people. Confident in his ability to find his way home, he set out.

The shortened days of autumn brought with them cooler temperatures which dropped even more sharply after sunset. At night, cold and uncomfortable despite several hours of arduous slogging, Peder gathered boughs around him and settled in. The branches of fir and spruce managed to take the edge off the cold somewhat. Yet, clad only in his deerskin, he still felt chilled and slept very little.

He was hungry as well. The handfuls of partridgeberries he had found along the way were not enough to satisfy his hunger and lay heavy on his stomach. And to make matters worse, his feet were raw and blistered from his long walk.

When he stirred in the morning, stiff, sore, still cold, and facing the prospect of another day of hard travel, he was tempted to settle back into the boughs and stay there. He knew, however, that to do so would only delay his progress. Steeling himself for what he had to do, he arose.

With his thoughts now focused fully on his destination, he no longer worried about the skraelings on his trail. Indeed, in retrospect, he wondered if they had even bothered to search for him at all, if they would have broken off from the hunt just to follow him. The hunt, so essential to their survival, was infinitely more important than a captive like him. Indeed, the loss of one of their canoes would have been considered far more serious.

The birch, aspens, and alders were beginning to shed their leaves, and the wilderness was ablaze with their reds, oranges, and yellows. This signal that winter was looming was not lost on Peder and instilled in him an even greater sense of urgency. He kept a constant lookout for food, finding scattered patches of partridgeberries and, in one instance, a small patch of blueberries in a sheltered area not yet touched by frost.

Much of the land he faced was open barrens, and he was able to make relatively good progress. The forests that sometimes confronted him were much more difficult, so he tried to skirt them, veering constantly toward the coastline, where he was often forced to traverse the headlands or pick his way along the rocky coastline itself.

Progress over the next few days was slow, painstaking slogging on feet that were so raw and sore he could scarcely put them to the ground. Sharp hunger gnawed constantly at the pit of his stomach, and his body was battered by the bitter winds that blew relentlessly. Peder knew he was growing weaker by the day. Unable to find the nourishment his body needed for the arduous task he had undertaken, he sometimes despaired of ever reaching his destination. Still, every step brought him that much closer to the settlement and his people, and this knowledge gave him the perseverance to keep plodding onward.

On the ninth day, late in the afternoon, he found himself on a high rise overlooking a beach, and he realized that it was the beach where the massacre of Ralf and the others had taken place. He scanned it for signs of their bodies, but scavengers or tides, or both, had done their work well, and there was no evidence that such a terrible event had ever unfolded there. There was no sign of the knarr

either. He wondered if Bjoern had survived the attack and sailed it
away. Or had he too been killed and the knarr taken away by the tides?
Still, he felt heartened by the sight of the beach, for it confirmed his
position and he knew that the settlement lay just a few more days away.

Thus encouraged, he set forth again. Three days later, by now
extremely weak and at times light-headed and disoriented, Peder saw
in the distance a headland that looked familiar to him. Behind it, he
knew, was the settlement. He was almost home. One more day, two at
the most. He knew he could make it now.

When he finally approached the settlement he felt tears coursing
down his face. Unseemly behaviour for a Norseman, he knew, and he
tried to stem them before anybody saw him. He was home, that was all
that mattered.

Yet, even from a distance, he sensed that something was wrong.
It was too quiet. No smoke rose from the longhouse and there was
no sign of activity. The place was deserted.

The door of the longhouse hung awry on broken hinges, and
when he entered the building it was cold and damp – and empty.
He saw that the place where he had always slept had been taken over
by mice. Their litter and droppings indicated that they had been there
for some time.

He didn't know what to do. Where had his people gone? Would
they ever be coming back? Had Bjoern, the man left on the knarr
when Ralf and the others had gone ashore, somehow escaped and
managed to bring the knarr back here by himself? Had he then taken
the others away?

Overwhelmed with despair, Peder felt helpless. He let himself
succumb to the desire to simply slip to the floor and drift off into
oblivion.

The night passed, and morning found him alone on the dirt floor
of the longhouse. The sun was well overhead before he stirred to
face the day, beset by abject hopelessness. The flame which had brought

him this far had been extinguished. Finally hunger forced him to rise, and he searched the settlement. In the small garden where his mother and some of the other women had always planted a few vegetables, he found a handful of small potatoes and a few partially eaten out turnips. These paltry remnants were the gleanings of the main crop that his people must have taken with them when they left. It wasn't much but it might keep him alive for a few more days.

Nourished by the potatoes and turnips, he felt a little stronger. He spent the rest of the day wandering aimlessly around the settlement, discovering that his people had taken everything of value with them. He found only a small piece of sail canvas which he thought he might use to cover himself to help ward off the cold at night. Late in the afternoon he gathered boughs and sticks and erected a rough shelter a short distance from the longhouse. He could not abide another night alone in the longhouse. He feared that the ghosts of Ralf and the others would grant him no peace.

The next five days saw him scavenging for food and scanning the ocean for the presence of a large black sail. He'd eaten the few vegetables he had found, and most of the berries had, by then, withered with the cold temperatures and fallen to the ground. His main source of food now was the small trout that populated the little stream that ran through the settlement. He found it very difficult to catch them with only his hands, and he ate them raw, especially savouring the roe he found inside them.

In those five days Peder's strength gradually returned to the point where he no longer felt exhausted and faint most of the time. The blisters on his feet had healed and hardened, and he could walk again without pain. Yet, notwithstanding these improvements, he had finally come to accept the reality that he was all alone – perhaps the only human being for hundreds of miles around – and that without the others and the cooperative effort that had enabled the settlement to survive in this harsh land, he would surely die. He could not survive a winter alone.

On the morning of the sixth day, he opened his eyes. During the night he had dreamed about his mother. Her smiling face had watched over him, and her gentle hands had caressed his cheeks as they had done when he was a small child. He awoke resolute and uplifted. The instinct of survival had been rekindled. Peder knew what he had to do.

He faced south and steeled himself for another journey. With only the piece of sail canvas, he set forth once again – to retrace the steps that had brought him here. With the snow season looming, he knew he had to make haste. Without hesitation, he took the first step on his second trek, an undertaking that would prove to be infinitely harder and longer than the first.

Fifteen days into his journey, eight days after passing the beach of the massacre again, his strength began to fail, and for every hour he walked, he rested and slept threefold. He was constantly cold, even with both the sail canvas and his deerskin covering his body. At night he thought that he would surely freeze to death, and awoke several mornings to find the ground dusted with light snow or covered with hoar frost. His only food now was small trout from the brooks and streams he passed along the way. The berries that had sustained him for so long had since dried up. He was slowly dying on his feet, and each step forward was extremely painful.

On the twentieth day, he stopped and knelt to drink from a small pool. The face that looked back at him from the clear water was not his own. The gaunt haggard look, the haunted eyes, the sunken cheeks, the tangle of long red hair, and the red stubble covering the face were those of a stranger. He looked at his hands and saw, for the first time, that they were mere talons. He rolled up his sleeves and saw that his arms were like sticks. He felt his legs, and they were just as skeletal.

Peder knew that he could go no farther that day. He would rest here and try again tomorrow – if he could. He crawled into the shelter of a nearby copse of stunted spruce, covered himself with the sail canvas, and within minutes was fast asleep.

When he awoke hours later it was dark, and small snowflakes were falling gently from the night sky. As exhausted as he was, the events that had ensued in the seven months following his capture were vivid in his mind. How far had he come? He had long since lost track of the days. He wondered where his mother was. Was she still alive somewhere? He thought of Ralf and the others, Kjell, Bjoern, Gunner. Lastly, he thought of Asbut, his adopted brother, the skraeling boy who had transcended fear and hatred to befriend him.

Then, as he was drifting back to sleep, he thought he smelled smoke. He wasn't certain, and waited. Again the hint of wood smoke passed his nostrils, faint but unmistakable this time. It meant people, undoubtedly skraelings. Maybe Asbut's own tribe.

When Peder awoke the next morning, snow lay heavy on the ground. Sleep had done little to restore his strength, and he lay stiff, cold and sore in his shelter, still utterly exhausted. For an hour he tried to move, but couldn't summon the strength to rise to his feet. The smell of smoke still lingered in the morning air, and he knew that if he could only rise he might be able to track it to its origin. Finally, by sheer power of will, he managed to get to his feet and take his first tentative step.

Three hours later he arrived at the encampment. They all stood motionless, even the children, watching him in silence as he staggered into the clearing. He stumbled toward Asbut's mamateek, willing himself to remain conscious and stay on his feet for a few more minutes. Asbut waited there, as still as the others.

Finally Peder faced Asbut, close enough to touch him. He leaned forward until he rested his forehead against Asbut's. "Brother," he said.

He started to fall. Strong hands grabbed him, hands that were   89
compassionate and caring – hands of forgiveness.

Then, before he lost consciousness, he whispered, "Peder is home. Peder is skraeling now."

In 1960, Norwegian explorer Helge Ingstad and his wife Anne Stine Ingstad, an archaeologist, discovered the remains of a small Viking settlement at L'Anse aux Meadows on the northernmost tip of Newfoundland's Northern Peninsula. It was named a World Heritage Site by UNESCO in 1978. Archaeologists have determined that the settlement dates from around 1000 AD. L'Anse aux Meadows has been authenticated as the only known Norse site in North America. This is the setting for the fictional story "The Skraeling." Information in the story is based on Joseph R. Smallwood's *Encyclopedia of Newfoundland and Labrador* (St. John's: Newfoundland Book Publishers Limited, 1967, 1981) and *The Dictionary of Newfoundland English*, edited by G. M. Story, W. J. Kirwin, and J. D. A. Widdowson (Toronto: University of Toronto Press, 1982).

THE DRUNK

"My Blessed Virgin, I just can't believe it. Wouldn't the likes of him make you sick to your stomach?" Agnes O'Brien's disgust was as evident in her face as it was in her words.

"Yes," agreed her friend, Rita Shea. "What a state of a human being! And to think that there might be a poor wife and youngsters somewhere waiting for him to bring home a bit of food and God knows what else. What a shame!"

"Oh well," added Agnes. "It should make us appreciate the ones we've got, I suppose, as bad as they are."

The indignant women veered out into the street, giving the drunk a wide berth as they scurried past.

Three days earlier their words would have meant very little to him. He would have ignored them, if indeed, he heard them at all.

But today they stung, hurt more deeply than he could have imagined. For Roddie Murphy was sober – and he didn't like it. Three days of abstinence had left him with the shakes, and he was contemplating what he might do about them. Perhaps he would try to track down Gertie; she was sure to have a drop of what he needed.

It was all the fault of that Salvation Army lady. He didn't know who she was, had never even seen her before, but he had recognized the uniform she wore immediately. Slouched against the front of the building,

minding his own business and feeling no pain, he had known nothing
until she had him on his feet and had launched into her tirade.
He couldn't remember much of what she said. It was mostly just a
jumble now, but some small part of it had penetrated his foggy brain
and triggered some long-lost sense of conscience. Perhaps it was the
part where she had said, "The world's worse sinner, even a drunken sot
like you, can be redeemed and gathered into the arms of our blessed
Saviour if you repent and change your ways. And if you don't change
your ways, my man, you're doomed to roast in hell with the very worst
of them."

Whatever it was, she had scared him. At one point he had
thought she was going to strike him, she looked so angry. She could
have gotten away with it, too, he knew, because his own puny body
would have been no match for her brawny frame. She had left him
trembling on the sidewalk, resolved that he would give what she said
a try. Now he wasn't so sure. Sobriety certainly had its downside.

Still, he lingered there on the street, postponing his search for
Gertie, deterred by an image of the Salvation Army lady that was
still sharp in his mind. He was hungry and hoped that a few of the
passersby might find enough compassion in their hearts to drop a
copper or two into the cap he had laid out before him.

He stayed there for the rest of the day, until dark, and then left to
wend his way to Victoria Park where he would nestle himself away in
his favourite nook for the night. He knew that his hunger would not
be assuaged that evening, for his cap was still as empty as when he had
placed it on the ground hours earlier.

Snug in his bower, he slept fitfully for a short while until the
hunger pangs gnawing at his stomach woke him. He was still "on the
rats" and knew that to stay where he was would be to spend several
sleepless hours in hunger and extreme discomfort. He decided to leave
for the waterfront. Perhaps some late-arriving vessel might be a source
of something to eat. It was now three o'clock in the morning.

He headed east on Water Street. Passing the railway station, he was tempted to go in and try to pass the night, but he had been kicked out so many times before that he knew it was useless to attempt it. He drank from the public fountain at the bottom of Alexander Street. Water Street was deserted, a far cry from the bustle and din of day. Very few sounds disturbed the stillness of the early morning hours. He paused in front of the Haberdashery, where, by the glow of the streetlight, he sized up the merchandise on display. He wondered what it would be like to have the money to go in and buy a suit or whatever else he wanted. He ambled on. Near Beck's Cove, he felt the need to relieve himself and ducked into an alleyway. A rat scurried beneath his feet. He kicked at it and sent it squealing into the darkness.

As he stood there, he noticed small shimmers of light dancing on the building on the west side of the alley. He thought he must be seeing things. Then he smelled smoke. Returning to the front of the buildings, he peered in through the windows, firstly the building to the west and then the other. Fire! He started to flee. If he was caught there, they might blame him for starting it.

Then he heard screaming from somewhere above him. By the sound of the voice, it was a woman. Her frantic screams told him that she must be trapped. Again he started to leave: it was none of his business. But he was stopped short by the same flicker of conscience the Salvation Army lady had aroused. He had to do something. But what?

He seized an ash can and hurled it at the window, shattering it into fragments. He stepped through, careful to avoid the flames and the jagged shards. His hands searched the wall for a light switch. Finding it quickly, he flipped it on but only a single light somewhere in the back of the room lit up. In the dim light and smoke, he spotted the door leading to the staircase, but when he opened it, a fiery downdraft knocked him backward. He fled outside.

Was there another way into the premises? He went behind the
building, searching for a back door, but flames were already licking at
the frame. Then he spotted a scaffold thirty feet above his head – and
a long spindly ladder leading up to it. It was his only chance.

He started to climb, his legs trembling. Halfway up, his fear
of heights forced him to stop. With a great effort of will, he pushed
his fear aside and continued upward. With each rung he passed, the
ladder bent and swayed. He prayed that it was fastened at the top.
When he finally reached the scaffold, he stepped gingerly onto it.
It gave beneath his feet and he feared it might break under his weight.
He held his breath. Then, on hands and knees, he crept toward the
only window in the rear of the building.

He called through the open window, "Is anyone there?"

No answer.

He called again, as loudly as he could. He shouted until he was
certain he was in the wrong place or that the woman who had
screamed had succumbed to the smoke and flames.

He was creeping back to the ladder when he heard a feeble
"Help me, someone." Turning, he saw the face of a terrified young
woman at the open window.

"Take him. Please. Save him," she pleaded. She passsed a small
squirming bundle into his outstretched arms.

"You're coming too," he shouted. "Just follow me."

Holding the baby tightly under his left arm, he crept back to the
ladder. She followed him. The scaffold groaned under their weight.

"Don't look down," he instructed. "Just stay tight to me."

They navigated their way to the ladder. He felt the weight of the
infant. How would he get onto the ladder with the baby in his arms?

"Wait til I get started, and then get on yourself and climb down
behind me. You can do it."

He steeled himself for the transfer to the ladder. The baby squirmed under his arm and for a second or two he thought he was going to drop it. He recovered, and when his feet were firmly planted on the topmost rungs, he held on to calm himself for the descent. With the young woman gamely following, his probing feet found the rungs, one after another, until, eventually, he felt the firm earth. Depositing the baby on the ground, he reached up and helped the young woman down the last few rungs.

She snatched up her child and held him tightly to her body.

He pulled them away from the building. "There, there," he comforted. "You're safe now. It's all over, so get along with ye before that old building falls down on top of you."

He heard sirens. The firemen were on their way.

He needed a drink. To hell with the Salvation Army lady. He had to find Gertie.

On Sunday morning, Agnes O'Brien and Rita Shea made their way to the West End to attend morning mass at St. Patrick's.

"You must have got some shock," Rita probed, eager for the details even though she had heard most of it before.

"Rita, my dear, I couldn't believe it when they brought Anne Marie and the baby over to my place like that in the middle of the night. All blackened, they were, and the stink of smoke on their clothes enough to drive you outdoors. Poor Anne Marie was beside herself for hours. Wouldn't put little Timmy out of her arms, she wouldn't. Poor little darling.

"I feel so guilty," she continued. "I should never have let her go to live in that old flat over the store in the first place. I can see now it was nothing but a firetrap, and with John away on the boat most of the time ... well I just can't think about it."

"Oh well, they're safe enough now," Rita said. "And that's all that matters." Then she added, "I wonder who it was who went up and got them out? Perhaps we'll never find out."

"Yes, maid," Agnes replied. "I'd love to know that too. Anne Marie says she's certain she's seen the man around someplace but can't remember where. I would like nothing better than to meet him face to face myself and tell him how much I owe him. He must be a saint."

"Well, they say God sends his angels to help us out in our times of trouble." Rita slowed and grabbed Agnes' arm. "Look, there's that old drunk again, and on a Sunday morning too. It's disgusting."

Stepping nimbly to avoid Roddie Murphy's outstretched legs, she continued, "They should get the likes of that off the streets and put them away somewhere where they can't bother decent people."

"Yes," agreed Agnes. "If they did that this city would certainly be a much better place, wouldn't it?"

AUTHOR'S NOTE

St. John's, like most cities and towns, has always had its share of *characters* known for the oddness or extreme nature of their actions. The public view of such individuals typically ranged from amusement to tolerance to aversion or disgust. Very few people, however, ever truly endeavoured to get to know the real persons living within some of these strange men and women. They were generally dismissed as oddballs or outcasts. This fictional story "The Drunk" is based on the true inner character of one such individual.

THE FUGITIVE

He knew they were coming for him. He had known it long before they rounded the point and came his way. He knew it before the two boats, each with four men aboard, had come ashore so close to him that he could hear their voices, even though he did not understand a word of what they said. Calmly accepting the inevitable, he had made no attempt to flee. In his weakened state he could never have outdistanced them anyway. His only option was to hide until they left again. He was confident that he was safe in his concealment. He had chosen it well, a small impenetrable haven. His only fear was that his coughing sickness might betray him should they come too close. Having already hidden there for hours, his legs were now stiff from squatting on his haunches and pain racked his emaciated body. He knew that in order to survive, he might have to endure yet another long period of discomfort.

He watched as the white men searched the cove and the hills surrounding it. One of them came so close that he could smell the man's stinking body, and it sickened him. The man had paused scant feet away, suspicion written on his face, before shrugging and moving on again. They stayed there most of the day. Having satisfied themselves that the place was deserted, they lit a fire on the beach and cooked themselves a meal, after which they rested and drank, passing two jugs back and forth. For a while, he worried they were going to stay for the night and was relieved when they finally boarded their boats and started paddling out as the sun began its descent toward the horizon.

Still, despite his discomfort, he remained in his hiding place and waited, emerging only when the last vestiges of daylight streaked the western sky and he was certain that his antagonists were well away. He could scarcely move. His body refused to obey him. It took enormous effort to take the few faltering steps to the sandy beach below. There he rested again until the moon came up and he was able to continue on his way. He knew where he was going. It was not far.

He awoke the next morning to gentle, refreshing raindrops falling on his face. He went to the lake and drank deeply of its cool morning water. Although he had not eaten anything in days, he did not feel the need for food. He knew that his wasted body would have rejected it in any case. The rustling of the breeze in the birch trees and the barely audible sound of wavelets lapping against the shoreline calmed him. The calm pushed the events of the previous day from his mind. He surveyed his surroundings, the spectrum of autumn colours which stretched as far as he could see and the shimmering early morning blueness of the lake – his beloved lake – which had sustained him and his extended family for so long. The beauty of the morning stirred up images of similar autumn days long past when he and his people had been able to live there in peace.

Now, the sandy shoreline bore no evidence of the mamateek[6] in which he and his wife and children had once lived, or of the other mamateeks which had stretched out along this part of the lake in happier times. They had long since been dismantled and their parts destroyed or hidden to deny the ever-encroaching white men any knowledge of their existence.

---

[6] Mamateek is the Beothuk word for wigwam or living place. They were constructed of layers of birch bark spread over a frame of fir poles with a hole in the centre of the roof from which smoke could escape.

The people were all gone now, having succumbed to the coughing sickness and starvation, and the brutality of the furriers, the white men who had infiltrated their wilderness and destroyed their way of life. He did not know if any of his people still lived. If they did, he did not know who, or where they might now be. The last of his people that he'd had contact with was his cousin Shanawdithit and her mother and older sister. All three, ridden with the coughing sickness, had surrendered into the custody of the whites, preferring the indignity of captivity to the death and horrific suffering that had surrounded them for so long. They had wanted him to come with them, but he refused. He could never, no matter how desperate his own circumstances, bring himself to live for even a single day in a white man's world.

He spent the day on the shore of the lake, sleeping as much as possible to avoid the pain and the frequent bouts of coughing that racked his body and to try to forget for a few minutes his loneliness and anguish. As darkness approached, he drank once more from the lake before retiring to the edge of the woods for the night.

For a few hours he slept the deep sleep of the un-damned, a fleeting respite from his suffering. Around midnight, when the moon was high, he awoke to see a brilliant succession of shooting stars blaze their way across the night sky. The stars stirred memories of the nights he had watched them as a boy from that very same spot. Those were better times. He remembered the annual canoe trips down the rivers to the great water where the tribe took all the salmon and shellfish they wanted and brought them back to the lake to sustain them through the long winter months. He remembered his part in herding the caribou along miles of sapling fences that his people had cleverly erected to drive the animals into the narrow pass where the hunters could easily kill them with their arrows and lances. He remembered the quarters of caribou meat that had hung over smoking charcoals and how the women scraped and chewed the hides to incredible softness. He also remembered his participation in daring raids to steal and damage the property of the white settlers along the coast. He recalled fondly the night he and five others from his tribe had hidden in their canoe under the wharf of the white chief while angry fishermen trod only inches above their heads. It was the night they had set adrift the white chief's boat with its summer's load of salted salmon.[7]

Those times were long gone now. His thoughts turned to the times that had followed – the bad times. He shuddered as he remembered being awakened one cold spring morning by a large number of white men who had unexpectedly crept upon him and his family and the others as they slept, surrounding their mamateeks and ordering them out into the frigid morning air. He could never forget the sequence of events that had ensued that day. The sight of his aunt, Demasduit, being manhandled and dragged away by the white intruders was forever etched in his memory, as was the horror of her husband Nonosbawsut, the leader of their small tribe, being stabbed and bludgeoned to death as he desperately tried to wrestle her from their grasp. The despair that followed had been unbearable, made even worse by the death of Demasduit's motherless baby three days later.

Life before that had been difficult enough for him and his people. They had long since been cut off from their traditional routes to the coastal waters which they needed for access to the seafood and other marine resources that nourished and supported them. They were now forced to survive primarily on the trout of the lake and the plants surrounding it. Even their access to the caribou herds had been virtually eliminated. White man's diseases had left many of his people too maimed and weakened to carry on any semblance of normal life. After Demasduit's capture and the slaying of Nonosbawsut, life became infinitely worse. Fear and the ever-present danger from the growing population of white people drove them even farther into hiding and a subsistence of utter, abject misery.

---

[7] This raid by the Beothuk occurred on the property of John Peyton, Jr., renowned salmon merchant and magistrate from Exploits, Notre Dame Bay.

Memories still flooded his mind when the first hint of light appeared in the east and tiny songbirds began their trilling to herald the advent of another day. Suddenly, a particularly violent paroxysm of coughing seized his body and he retched uncontrollably. Blood gushed from his mouth and soaked the front of his garment and the ground around him. He tried to drag himself farther into the bushes but could not.

Then he saw them coming. He was not afraid. For the first time in a long, long while, peace filled his mind, and he was happy. The ancestors had come to claim him, to escort him to *Theehone*.[8] His ordeal was finally over. They beckoned and he went to them.

---

[8] Theehone is the Beothuk word for the afterlife. It is believed that the Beothuk honoured the sun and the moon. An origin myth suggests that the Beothuk race sprang from an arrow from the sky that stuck into the earth and transformed itself into human form.

AUTHOR'S NOTE

Shanawdithit is generally acknowledged to be the last member of the Beothuk race. It is highly probable, however, that at the time of her surrender to the white settlers in 1823 there was still a small number of other Beothuk survivors who remained in the wilderness to fend for themselves. Joseph R. Smallwood's *Book of Newfoundland* (St. John's: Newfoundland Book Publishers Limited, 1967) reinforces this point with a reference to the finding of two drowned Beothuk men subsequent to Shanawdithit's surrender. The Beothuk character in this fictional story could have been one such individual.

MAGGIE'S LAMENT

aggie's tea sat cold in her cup and her tea biscuit lay untouched on the table. The stove fire had burned down hours earlier and the chill of the night air infiltrated the house, bringing with it dampness and discomfort. Still, she continued to sit at the kitchen table, staring into nothingness and dreading the thought of going up to bed for yet another night of sleeplessness. She was grieving, and had been for a long while.

Her sorrow was rooted in time, more than ten years, and increasingly overwhelmed her with each passing day. She could see no end to it, and no longer knew how to deal with it, for her profound sadness was not a grief one normally associates with death, loss, or sickness. That, she could have dealt with. Indeed, many years earlier she had coped with the loss of her husband, William, mourned his passing, and gotten over his death to resume raising their children. Time had eased the pain. She still remembered, though, and kept the treasured memories of their life together in a special and private chamber of her heart.

Her all-consuming sorrow now was for the living and the healthy – her own three sons: Albert, Charlie, and Fred, the pride of her life and the centre of her existence. Having reared them mostly on her own, she had seen them blossom from babies into lusty, vibrant boys filled with energy and life. At times she had wondered where she might get the strength and energy herself to keep up with them. Sadly, they were now the cause of her grief. For the three boys, who had been each other's best friends, who had played together and stood up for and protected each other against all perils, had grown apart. Adults now, with wives and children of their own, they no longer spoke to each other. In their tiny village, they were strangers, passing on the road without as much as a nod of recognition. Their wives, too, didn't associate with each other because their husbands discouraged them from doing so. The estrangement had even descended to their children, and though some of them were in the same grades in school, they never played together.

Maggie knew what was at the root of her sons' bitterness toward each other. It was the piece of bottom land her husband had left at his death. It was one of the few arable fields in the area, and therefore a valuable piece of property. William had not designated an heir to this land, so it simply remained in the family as a place to plant a few crops. The trouble began when Charlie, nearing the age of twenty-five and about to be married, laid claim to the field. As the oldest son, he deemed it his birthright. Albert and Fred, not much younger than Charlie and contemplating marriage themselves, disagreed and challenged his right to the property. They argued that the field should somehow be left to the benefit of them all. Their initial arguments and attempts to resolve the issue failed, and their discussions quickly turned to hostility and recriminations. The tension escalated. Every time one of them passed by the field, the sight of it only served to drive the wedge deeper. Consequently, the field had been left fallow while the three brothers went their own obstinate ways.

While Maggie knew the cause of her sons' estrangement, she couldn't understand it. It was alien to her concept of family. To her, family transcended all grievances and counted above everything else. Bloodlines meant life-long love and connection no matter what transpired. On the few occasions when she tried to intervene, she had been gently rebuffed.

Maggie herself was not part of the estrangement, for each of her sons came to visit her on a regular basis, making sure to avoid each other when they came. Her daughters-in-law and her grandchildren visited her regularly as well. For that, she was grateful, but it wasn't enough. She wanted them all to be a real family again.

Finally, shortly after midnight, the kitchen had become too cold for her to stay, and she reluctantly made her way upstairs. She said her prayers, got into bed hoping that she might be able to sleep, and leaned over to blow out the lamp on her bed-table. She changed her mind. Getting out of bed again, she went to her bureau and drew out of its lower drawer an old scribbler, one in which she had been jotting down her thoughts for some time. The scribbler was her release, a channel when her grief simply had to have an outlet – like tonight. She wrote for a while and then laid the scribbler down on the bed beside her. She extinguished the lamp.

Maggie slept fitfully, waking frequently enough to hear the clock downstairs chime each passing hour. She tried to focus her thoughts on other, more pleasant things, but invariably, after a few minutes, they strayed back to her troubles. Then, just as the first faint light of dawn was easing into the darkness of the room, she felt tightness in her chest, then hard pain. She tried to sit up, but couldn't. She couldn't breathe. Suddenly brightness filled the room, and she cried out. Her body shuddered, and then relaxed. Maggie, at the age of sixty-eight, had drawn her last breath.

The next day, when Charlie's wife, Mary-Anne, noticed that Maggie's clothesline was empty on washday, they decided to check on her. Both felt uneasy, half expecting to find Maggie feeling unwell, but they certainly did not expect to find her dead. The coldness of her flesh told them she had lain there for some time.

"I'll go for the minister," Charlie said. "Do you mind staying here with her until I get back?"

"You go on, I'll be okay." Although Mary-Anne thought it would be better if he went to tell his bothers instead, she held her tongue. They'd find out soon enough.

While Charlie was gone she combed her mother-in-law's hair, washed her face, and tried to rearrange her clothing. It was then that she spotted the scribbler, which had lain concealed under the blanket. The dog-eared cover was creased and faded with age. The date pencilled in on the cover was September 16, 1938, nine years earlier.

She started to read. At first glance, the writing was illegible. Indecipherable spidery scrawls, like those of a small child, seemed to have been placed at random across the pages. Mary-Anne put down the scribbler and began to tidy up the room, trying to keep herself busy until Charlie and the minister arrived. Curiosity piqued, she picked up the scribbler again.

She studied the first page until eventually, despite the poor hand-writing, misspellings, and the lack of capitalization and punctuation, she was able to make some sense of it. *life shoodnt be like this ... cant stand it.* Mary-Anne was turning the page to read more when she heard the door downstairs open and the voices of Charlie and the minister. She tucked the scribbler inside her sweater.

Two days later, Charlie, Albert, and Fred buried their mother. Although they carried her coffin into the church together, they did not speak to each other. Indeed, during the entire waking period and the funeral itself, they exchanged words only when absolutely necessary. When Maggie was interred, the brothers and their families returned to their homes without even saying goodbye.

Over the course of the next few days, whenever she had a few minutes alone, Mary-Anne continued her perusal of Maggie's scribbler. Gradually the innermost workings of her mother-in-law's mind, documented over the years, became clear. *taring me apart ... childern not noing there famly ... my falt ... killing me.*

By the time she finished reading, Mary-Anne realized the depth of the woman's grief. Maggie had died of a broken heart. Her sons' alienation from each other had killed her. Mary-Anne was sure of it.

At the oddest times, passages from Maggie's scribbler would flash through her mind, nagging at her conscience: *sadness ... dont no wut to do ... wish the Lord wud jus take me.* Mary-Anne's heart was heavy with the knowledge that her mother-in-law had suffered in silence. What should have been her golden years had, instead, been a time of great sadness and torment. The daughter-in-law was torn by what she had read, and wondered what she should do. How would Charlie react if he knew? she wondered. Would he be angry or resentful? Would it make any difference?

She decided to show Charlie his mother's scribbler.

Mary-Anne picked her moment: Sunday morning, when everyone else would be in church. "I don't feel well," she told him. "I don't think I can go this morning. Perhaps you can stay home with me."

Charlie, although surprised, agreed.

When the children were sent off, she sat him at the kitchen table and handed him the scribbler. "Read this. It belonged to your mother."

He opened it to the first page, looked at it for a few minutes, riffled through the rest of the pages, and handed it back to her. "I can't read this. It just looks like a lot of hen scratches to me. What is it, anyway?"

"Can I read it to you?" Looking down at the scribbler, she read aloud, slowly, "I wish Charlie knew how much this is hurting me, but if I say anything they might all stop talking to me."

Mary-Anne looked up. "Would you like me to go on?" She fully expected him to say he'd heard enough. Instead, he nodded.

"I wish with all my heart they could be like they were when they were little boys," she read. Mary-Anne glanced up and saw tears running down her husband's face.

By the time she'd finished reading the last page, Charlie realized the depth of his mother's despair. How could he have been oblivious to his mother's pain and sorrow all these years? In the midst of her family, she had suffered so greatly, and none of them had known it. Worse still, he knew he had been the cause of it. And now it was too late, she was gone.

Guilt and regret, blame and responsibility filled his mind. He considered the piece of fallow bottom land that had come between him and his brothers, and in a moment of brutally honest reflection, acknowledged that ownership of that small bit of land had been unimportant. Despite slight for slight, hurt for hurt, the matter could have been resolved with a bit of give and take, but had, instead, been left to fester: ten years of animosity and hardheartedness. He realized, too, the wrong he had visited upon his wife and his children. Mary-Anne should have been able to enjoy the company of her sisters-in-law all these years, and his children's right to know and be friends with their own first cousins should not have been denied to them. Charlie felt shame and remorse.

Although he knew it might be too late, he decided he would try to make things right between him and his brothers. He would approach Albert first. Charlie didn't know what he would say, but hoped that, when they actually met face to face, the right words would come.

The following Sunday, when Charlie spotted Albert walking home from church alone, he decided this would be the moment. Apprehensive, he called to him, "Wait up, Albert. I want to talk to you."

Albert stopped in his tracks but didn't turn around. Charlie walked round to face him and saw the question marks in his brother's eyes. Was there something else there too, Charlie wondered, wariness, perhaps contempt?

Having come this far, Charlie suddenly found it difficult to proceed. How could he swallow his pride and what could he say that would undo the wrong of the past several years?

Steeling himself, he forged ahead. "Albert," he said, "Mother's death has made me realize how short and uncertain life is." He paused to catch his breath. "It's made me see things in a different light. About the piece of bottom land, I can see now that I was wrong on that."

He stopped, then forced himself to go on. "Maybe it isn't too late to fix it all up. What do you think?"

He saw the shock in Albert's eyes, and then, Charlie was certain, the faint hint of a smile. "Perhaps we could," his brother replied. "Yes, perhaps we could." And for the first time in nearly a decade the two of them walked along together.

"Albert, I'm thinking about building a bigger skiff and I need someone to go in on it with me. Interested?" Charlie added.

Later that day, they sought out Fred, and he, too, welcomed the chance to put the brotherly feud behind them. Indeed, his own feelings over the years had not been nearly as strong as Charlie's and Albert's, and he had often yearned for the opportunity for some sort of reconciliation.

A few days later, as Charlie and Albert were laying out the keel in the back cove, Fred showed up. "I heard you two were building a new boat."

"Yes, b'y," Charlie answered. "It's going to be a big one too. Plenty of room for three."

The following spring, when the frost had gone out of the ground and the earth on Maggie's grave had settled, the family gathered in the cemetery to erect her headstone and plant flowers on her grave. It was a family project, one in which every member took part, all eighteen of them. When it was almost done, Charlie stood back with Mary-Anne, marvelling at the sight. Quietly he said, "When me and Albert and Fred were working on the boat the other day, we talked about the piece of bottom land. We've decided to sell it and split the money. It won't amount to much anyway, and that way our own quarrel will never be reopened by our children."

108 He considered the newly planted rose bush on the grave. "I wish Mother could see this," he said. "It's a shame she'll never know."

Mary Anne smiled, realizing that, in death, Maggie had accomplished what she'd wanted so badly in the last ten years of her life.

"She knows, Charlie. I'm sure of it."

AUTHOR'S NOTE

Feuds have torn families apart and destroyed them since time began. For reasons that are sometimes difficult to comprehend, once loving and caring family members become pitted against each other – sibling against sibling, parent against child. Invariably there is a family member who suffers greatly because of such alienations. In this fictional story, Maggie, a long-suffering and grieving mother, is one of these individuals.

INDIAN KILLERS

*N*onosbawsut watched in wonder as the whitefaces rowed his father, Ashsut, his sister, his two younger brothers, and many other members of the tribe out to the two mamashees[9] which lay anchored a short distance offshore. He too had wanted to go, but by the time he got to the tapathooks[10] they had already been filled and there was no room for him. He was enthralled by the mamashees' strange shapes, the long poles that reached skyward from their decks, and above all else, their immense size. He had never seen anything even remotely like them before. He hoped that when the others were brought back, he would also have the opportunity to go out to examine one of them at close range and be able to explore its interior. Having gotten over his initial inhibitions toward the whitefaces, he felt eager and excited, and the small axe he had been given as a gift felt good in his hand. Little did he realize at that moment that he was witnessing the initiation of the persecution of his race that would continue unabated for the next three hundred and thirty years, until he and his people were eventually vanquished from the face of the earth.

---

[9] Mamashee is the Beothuk word for a large vessel. It is highly unlikely, however, that the Beothuk had ever seen anything as large as Corte-Real's ships before that time.

[10] Tapathook is the Beothuk word for canoe. Varying in length from sixteen to twenty-two feet, they were constructed of caribou skins sewed over a framework of laths and gunnels, and curved upward at each end.

The Beothuk Indians, Newfoundland's aboriginal people, were doomed to extinction from the moment the Venetian explorer, Giovanni Caboto, stepped ashore, allegedly at Bonavista, on June 24, 1497, and claimed the New Founde Lande for Henry VII, the king of England. There is no suggestion that Caboto himself or any of his crew inflicted any harm upon the native inhabitants or intimidated them in any manner. Indeed, there is no firm evidence to indicate that they even encountered any natives during their brief stay there. It was the wave of Europeans that followed in Caboto's wake that would initiate the carnage and brutality that would ultimately see the Beothuk nation driven to extinction.

It didn't take long for the persecution to begin. In 1500, just four short years after Caboto's landfall, King Manuel I of Portugal, encouraged by the discovery, sent his own explorers, Gaspar Corte-Real and his brother Miguel, westward in search of new territories and islands for Portugal. The Corte-Reals are thought to have reached Labrador sometime in 1501 before finally landing on the shores of Newfoundland later that same year. It is recorded that the Corte-Real brothers, unlike Cabot, did encounter Beothuk and managed to engage them in a friendly meeting, exchanging presents and sharing food with them. Having lulled the natives into their confidence, the Corte-Reals invited the Beothuk aboard their ships, the likes of which the natives had never seen and in which they showed great interest. Fifty-seven Beothuk, including most of Nonosbawsut's own family, took the brothers up on their invitation and were rowed out to the two Portuguese ships which lay anchored a short distance from the shore. The rest, waiting on the beach, were puzzled when the rowboats, after unloading their kinsmen, were lifted on board. Their confusion turned to disbelief and bewilderment when the sails of the vessels were unfurled and the two ships sailed away into the distance.

Once on board, the unsuspecting Beothuk were quickly over-powered by the Portuguese crews, shackled, and locked away below deck before they realized what was happening. They were taken back to

Portugal where the Corte-Real brothers presented them to King Manuel
as a gift. Some of the natives died before reaching Portugal. They were, perhaps, the fortunate ones. Several others who did survive the voyage were employed as slaves in King Manuel's court, while some, including Ashut, were put on display in carnivals and circuses throughout the country, where they were objects of ridicule and great curiosity. The captured Beothuk chieftain, if given the choice, would willingly have chosen death himself over the kind of life he was now forced to live.

It is believed that many of these Beothuk, removed from their natural environment and subjected to white man's diseases like small-pox, measles, and tuberculosis, died within a very short time, and that none of them lived very long in their captivity. Thus the Corte-Real brothers would, in effect, be the first of a long succession of persecutors who would eventually see the Beothuk race driven to extinction.

Because of the tragic circumstances of the capture of Nonosbawsut's people, he, having passed only twenty summers, suddenly found himself the leader of his tribe. With the loss of Ashut, their chieftain, and the other fifty-six members of the tribe who had been so cunningly spirited away, the remaining people instinctively turned to Nonosbawsut as their new chieftain. Their choice was based partly on the fact that Nonosbawsut was Ashut's son and his logical successor. It was prompted more so, though, by their recognition of the young man's ability to lead them through the difficult times ahead, for they realized that a new and terrible element had entered into their lives.

Nonosbawsut was equal to the task. Three attributes in particular marked him for the role. He was a natural leader, already wise in his ways, and he had learned much from his father. Secondly, he was extremely tall, towering well over the other men of his clan, and his strength and daring, despite his relatively young age, were already legendary. Lastly his eyes set him apart, unfathomable slate-grey pools which masked his emotions and lent him an air of aloofness and authority, and differentiated him from any other person in the tribe.

He led his tribe wisely until his death of natural causes eighteen years later. Under his guidance his people prospered and gradually recovered from the loss of so many of their members. Disciplined and resourceful, he made sure that they followed and respected the laws and ways of the ancestors, the ancient tenets that had sustained them for thousands of years, and when it was needed he meted out justice fairly and equitably. While he believed in and enforced the old ways, he had introduced one new cardinal rule: avoid the whitefaces at all costs. The kidnapping of his father and the others was never far from his mind and the ruthlessness he had observed that day had cemented his judgement of the white-skinned intruders.

His caution was well-founded, for that period saw the arrival of a succession of European ships which, following the lead of Gaspar and Miguel Corte-Real, came to Newfoundland's shores each year to capture Beothuk and bring them back to Europe as slaves. Several countries besides Portugal, including England and France, participated openly in this enterprise. The slave trade would undoubtedly have continued indefinitely but for one fact: the Beothuk people did not make suitable slaves. A chronicler of the time, Charlevoix, perhaps summed it up best when he said, "There is no profit at all to be obtained from the natives, who are the most intractable of men, and one despairs of taming them."[11] When that conclusion was reached by all concerned, the slave trade finally ceased. Nonosbawsut could be counted as perhaps the only Beothuk chieftain who had not lost a single person to this vile practise.

For more than a hundred years following Caboto's landfall, long after Nonosbawsut had passed on to the afterlife, permanent settlement in Newfoundland was prohibited. The fishing industry carried on in Newfoundland waters by England, France, Portugal, and Spain was strictly seasonal, with the fish-laden ships of these countries returning home to Europe each fall. During this period, contact between the Beothuk and the European fishermen appears to have been sporadic. The natives, wary because of their earlier experience at the hands of the

[11] James P. Howley, *The Beothucks or Red Indians*, p. 8

slave traders, avoided the Europeans and resisted most overtures made toward them for trading. They preferred instead to pilfer objects that interested them from the temporary fishing premises left behind each year by the Europeans. They were particularly attracted to anything made of iron, which could be melted and reshaped into other tools and implements.

Still, hostility did exist during this period, and there are many tales of bloody encounters and grisly acts of revenge and reprisal by both sides. Some historians, including noted Newfoundland politician and author Harold Horwood, assert that European fishermen routinely shot the native inhabitants on sight during these years, sometimes just for the sport of it. Despite this, however, there were also a number of successful attempts aimed at peaceful interaction between the Europeans and the Beothuk, although these seem to have invariably been negated by some subsequent hostile act of cruelty, all of which soured any lasting relationship between the groups.

It wasn't until 1610 that the first attempt to establish a permanent European presence in Newfoundland was undertaken when John Guy, a Bristol merchant, was authorized by the English government to found a colony at Cupers Cove (Cupids) in Conception Bay. In the fall of 1612, two years after he laid the foundation of his Seaforest Plantation in Cupids, Guy organized an expedition from his new settlement into adjoining Trinity Bay based on information he had received that Beothuk Indians resided there. After exploring Trinity Bay for some time, he and his party eventually came upon a deserted native village in the area now known as Spread Eagle, where they left gifts and presents before resuming their search. Several days later, in the location now named Sunnyside, Guy was surprised when his vessel was approached by two canoes carrying eight Beothuk men waving white flags and making friendly overtures.

Although Guy and his men were unaware of it, their activities had been monitored during the previous three days. Beothuk eyes had carefully scrutinized their every movement. Much discussion had taken place among the elders of the tribe to decide what course of action should be followed. The decision, after much deliberation, was finally reached to make contact with the white settlers. The Beothuk's covert observations had convinced most of the tribe's members that the intentions of the visitors were amicable and that an opportunity existed to establish a new relationship with them and end more than a century of hostility. Eighteen-year-old Edusweet, the great-great-great grandson of Nonosbawsut, had watched with great interest as the debate unfolded around the night fires. Because of his age, he was not encouraged to participate in the dialogue. His slate-grey eyes did not betray his excitement, but stories about the whitefaces, passed down through the generations, rang in his mind, and more than anything else he wanted to be in one of the canoes when contact was made.

A friendly encounter subsequently ensued between the Beothuk and the whites which lasted several days, during which the Europeans exchanged hatchets, knives, needles, and other items for Beothuk furs, and the two parties even shared a number of meals together. Edusweet, successful in his endeavour to be part of the welcoming party, partook of bread and butter for the first time in his life, and had at one point been able to shake the hand of the white chieftain himself. Looking into the eyes of the white leader, John Guy, he saw nothing but honesty, friendship, and respect.

Upon parting, Guy made arrangements with the Beothuk to meet them again at that same location the following year, and Edusweet, exhilarated by his encounter with the whitefaces, vowed that he would once again do everything in his power to be present for the occasion.

The next year, at the appointed time, an English ship did appear in the designated area of Trinity Bay. The excited Beothuk, including Edusweet, eager to meet Guy again, approached the vessel in their canoes only to be met by a hail of cannon fire. From his position in the rear canoe, Edusweet watched in horror and disbelief as the bodies of his uncle, Shebohut, and two others disintegrated in an explosion of blood and viscera. The captain of the ship, who was unaware of Guy's earlier meeting with the Beothuk and his commitment to meet them again, had thought that he and his crew were being attacked by the natives, and therefore opened fire. The Beothuk who were not slain fled, Edusweet among them, believing that they had been betrayed and deceived. This incident would virtually wipe out any chance of the Europeans ever establishing a lasting relationship with the Beothuk.

During the next century, the proliferation of European settlers arriving to set up permanent residence in Newfoundland, especially on the east and northeast coasts, made life for the Beothuk very difficult, and hostilities between the two groups escalated to new levels. Edusweet's descendants, having now to contend with the settlers while harvesting coastal food supplies such as salmon, codfish, mussels, and seabirds, frequently found themselves embroiled in bloody encounters with the newcomers. Stories of barbaric acts perpetrated against the Beothuk by the settlers and retaliatory scalpings and beheadings of whites by the natives abound during this period.

It was for this reason that Mamasut, the chieftain of the tribe at that time, assembled his people on a hill overlooking Trinity Bay one fine summer afternoon late in the seventeenth century. The yoke of leadership weighed heavily on his tall shoulders, and his intent was to tell his people that they would soon be leaving this area to go farther inland where they would be safer from their white tormentors. It was his intention, as well, to convene a telling, the traditional recounting of the stories of their past. By these measures he would be fulfilling his responsibility to ensure the safety of his people and guarantee that their history was passed on and preserved for future generations.

As the elders of the tribe spoke about their origins and the exploits of their ancestors, Mamasut listened as raptly as the youngest child there, and his grey eyes never once strayed from the speakers' faces. He was reliving the days of his ancestors. He was walking with his forebears, beside them every step of the way, lost in time.

Many of the stories told by the elders involved the whitefaces, for by then two hundred years of the Beothuk's own history was intrinsically entwined with the barbaric encounters with the strangers who had come to their shores. Perhaps the most chilling of the stories told that day was the Trinity Bay tradition that four hundred Beothuk were once herded out unto a long point of land, which afterwards became known as Bloody Point, in Hant's Harbour, where they were forced out into the water where every man, woman, and child was murdered by any means. As he listened, Mamasut could hear the screams of the victims and experience their anguish and terror as they were killed one by one in the bloodied sea. He had no way of knowing that within the space of three short years he too would become a victim of the white invaders.

The beginning of the eighteenth century saw little to improve the lot of Mamasut and his people or the rest of the island's aboriginal people. Right from the outset, in 1700, a man named Cull, along with five companions, set the tone for much of what was to follow. They left Notre Dame Bay early one morning, rounded Cape Freels in their small shallop, and entered Bonavista Bay. Then, following the coastline, they made their way southward until they eventually entered a long narrow inlet known today as Alexander Bay, one of the smaller bays situated in Bonavista Bay's southwest corner. The true purpose of their trip is unclear, but before it was over, it would result in an atrocity of the worse order.

When they reached the bottom of the inlet they went ashore near a location now known as Cull's Harbour, today a small community of a hundred people or so. Their intention was to explore the surrounding countryside. The area they were seeing for the first time was bountiful almost beyond imagination. The small bay, bounded on both sides by massive stands of spruce, fir, birch, and pine, boasted rivers that teemed with salmon and trout, and evidence of pine martin, otter, beaver, and other fur-bearing animals was everywhere. Cull and the others would have undoubtedly recognized the fishing, trapping, and logging potential of the area.

And then they discovered something else. There was strong

evidence of Beothuk habitation in the area. Cull and his men came across signs of the natives' existence in several locations. With that knowledge, a malicious thing came alive in Cull, and, forgetting everything else, he wanted to hunt them down and destroy them. The others may not have been as eager as Cull for the venture, but nevertheless went along with him as he pursued his cruel quest. Although there were five of them, they were intimidated by Cull, knowing well his explosive nature and his volatility when things did not go his way.

They scoured the bottom of the inlet for two full days, taking care not to give away their own presence lest they themselves be ambushed, and in the early morning hours of the third day their persistence was rewarded. They came upon a Beothuk encampment whose eight occupants were just rising for the day. When the surprised natives attempted to flee into the nearby woods, Cull opened fire. His companions, whether they had intended on being willing participants in the subsequent massacre, now had no choice, and their guns too took part in the assault. When the barrage was over, the eight Beothuk lay dead.

The massacre at that point was cruelly routine, this sort of thing had been carried out countless times. It was the grisly scene that followed that made this one infinitely worse. Cull insisted that the bodies be dragged to the shore and loaded onto the shallop. Once again his companions complied with his wishes, and when the vessel began its homeward journey, the eight corpses lay in a tangled heap in its stern. Then the sadistic Cull went to work.

Pulling one of the bodies from the pile, he took out his knife, ran it across the dead man's brow, cutting deep, and pulled the flesh and hair back until it came off in a bloody mess in his hand. Then he threw it overboard. In a similar manner, he desecrated the remaining seven bodies, cutting the throats of some of them as well, and mutilating others in unimaginably obscene ways. The wake of the shallop ran red with Beothuk blood. The other men, as hardened as they were, looked on in horror and disgust, nauseated by what they were witnessing. When Cull's gruesome act finally ended, he washed his hands and his knife in the sea, and sat back on the aft thwart and rested. One of the mutilated bodies left in his wake was that of Mamasut, the prudent chieftain who had led his people from Trinity Bay to this part of the island where they would be safer.

Mamasut and his family were just a few of the natives to die at the white settlers' hands. By that time hundreds of other Beothuk all around Newfoundland had fallen victim to the aggression of the ever-encroaching newcomers. The settlers had also brought with them diseases common to Europe, such as measles and tuberculosis, that had never before existed in Newfoundland, and countless natives succumbed to these new threats as well. And sometime during that century yet another nemesis entered the picture to make the Beothuk's existence even more tenuous. Mi'kmaq Indians, who during some earlier period had made their way from Nova Scotia to Newfoundland, and who had historically enjoyed good relations with the Beothuk, now became their enemy. This reputedly occurred because French fishermen from Newfoundland's west coast, plagued by theft and damage by the Beothuk of that region, conscripted the Mi'kmaq to their cause, armed them, and paid them a bounty for every Beothuk head they brought to them.

Wadawhegsut, the chieftain of a Beothuk tribe in the St. George's Bay area, was one of the first to find out about the treachery of their Mi'kmaq neighbours. One story recounts how a group of seven Mi'kmaq, travelling through Beothuk territory with the severed heads of a number of Beothuk hidden in their canoes, was invited by Wadawhegsut to partake of a feast with his people, traditional wilderness hospitality which the Mi'kmaq readily accepted. While the two groups were eating, some Beothuk children discovered the grisly contents of the canoes and informed their chieftain. Now wise to the Mi'kmaq's deed, Wadawhegsut strategically placed one of his own warriors between each visitor. At his signal, his men fell upon the unsuspecting visitors and stabbed them to death with their knives. From that day forward, hatred and open warfare existed between the two races which would end only with the Beothuk's eventual extinction.

Already beset on all fronts, the lot of the Beothuk people was soon to get worse – to deteriorate beyond their deepest fears. As European settlement proliferated and spread into Notre Dame Bay in the mid to late 1700s, the Beothuk were effectively denied access to their traditional coastal food resources and forced farther and farther back into the interior. Eventually, the entire Beothuk population, which some estimates place as low as three or four hundred by that time, ended up in the Red Indian Lake region at the head of the Exploits River.

The fur trade and the salmon fishery were by then flourishing in Notre Dame Bay, and increasing numbers of white settlers were attracted to the area to pursue these occupations. Valuable fur-bearing animals abounded in the forests of the region, and its rivers and streams teemed with the silver fish that the appetites of St. John's and Europe craved and demanded. In the eyes of many, there was only one impediment to the success of these important enterprises – the Beothuk. Furriers and fishermen alike routinely found their traps and nets stolen or damaged or their boats and premises and other properties destroyed. The elusive native raiding parties wreaking this havoc were difficult to catch, and the entrepreneurs of the area resorted to other means to protect their property. There is some contention that it was during this time, the late 1700s and early 1800s, that the slaying of Beothuk became systematic. The random and sporadic killing that previously existed gave way to something more deliberate and organized. Excursions into the interior, often organized under the pretext of recovering lost gear, were routinely planned and carried out, usually with fatal consequences for the Beothuk.

It was during these years, as well, that a breed of men openly called Indian Killers, plied their deadly profession. Most of these men were fur trappers by occupation, and their intimate knowledge of Notre Dame Bay's forests and wilderness areas enabled them to slaughter the native inhabitants whenever and wherever they encountered them. It is unclear whether these men operated on their own initiative or were employed by others for the task. Either way, the carnage they were able to inflict upon the already dwindling Beothuk population was enormous.

Included in this group were three men – Noel Boss, Old Man Rogers, and Tom Rousell – who together accounted for upwards of two hundred Beothuk deaths, possibly more. Boss openly boasted about his achievements, and kept count of his killings. His own stated objective was to kill an even one hundred Beothuk before he was through. Gender mattered little to him as he shot native men and women without distinction. Rogers, living near Twillingate at the time, admitted to killing "sixty or more of the savages," while Rousell killed indiscriminately at every opportunity.

Despite the extent of their carnage, the Indian Killers were probably relatively few in number. Most people in Notre Dame Bay at the time, in fact, considered their actions reprehensible and barbaric. John Peyton, Jr., the renowned salmon merchant and magistrate from Exploits who is recognized in Newfoundland history as a benefactor of the Beothuk, is believed to have been such an individual. Astonishingly though, his own father, John Peyton, Sr., is reputed to have openly participated in the persecution and butchery. It is alleged that Peyton, Sr., often accompanied excursions into the interior and that on one such occasion he was among those who slaughtered an encampment of twelve sleeping Beothuk whose mamateeks they stumbled upon. It is said that Peyton himself bludgeoned one of the defenceless natives with the stock of his gun until the walls of the mamateek were slick with the man's brains. Reports of his barbarity were so widespread and his reputation so fearsome that Magistrate John Bland of adjoining Bonavista Bay issued a standing order that Peyton never be permitted to set foot in any part of Bonavista Bay, and recommended that he should be ordered to leave the Bay of Exploits as well.

In 1810, the government of the day, which had hitherto turned a blind eye to the persecution of Newfoundland's aboriginal people, enacted laws to prevent further slaughter. The killing of Beothuk by white settlers was at last made a crime punishable to the full extent of the law. Finally awakened to the fact that the Beothuk race was on the verge of extinction, the government scrambled for ways to restore these people to some semblance of their former state. To achieve this, they employed a strategy of trying to capture a small number of native men and women to immerse them for a short while in the white man's culture, after which they would return them to their own people with the hope that they would assure their kinsmen of the government's good intentions toward them.

But it was too late. In 1819, the last of a number of ill-fated expeditions into the Red Indian Lake area, this one organized to recover stolen property and sanctioned by the government, would prove to be the dying gasp of a doomed race.

At that point in their demise, another Nonosbawsut was the chieftain of the few Beothuk still surviving. A twelfth generation descendant of his ancestral namesake, he would be the last chieftain of his race, the leader of a mere twenty-seven individuals, many of whom were riddled with tuberculosis and other diseases. Like his ancient predecessor, his main strategy was to avoid the furriers at all costs, and to that end he and his handful of followers led a nomadic existence, moving from place to place to escape detection.

On the clear morning of March 5, 1819, he was lying awake in his mamateek on the frozen surface of Red Indian Lake, near North East Arm, contemplating whether he should arise or stay a little longer. Lying beside him was his wife, Demasduit, with their infant daughter nestled to her breast. Although the sun had risen some hours before, he and his family and others in mamateeks nearby were taking refuge from the frigid temperature outside. It was a typical March morning, and by resting and sleeping for long periods of time, Nonosbawsut and his people were able to keep warm and conserve their waning strength and energy. Embers from the night fire still glowed, waiting to be blown upon and fanned once again into flames, and the usual early morning sounds brought a small measure of comfort to his troubled mind. The dire plight of his people was never far from his thoughts.

Then, as he began to doze again, his senses were alerted by something that didn't seem normal. Suddenly wide awake, he waited and listened, his nerves bristled and his body tensed. The small songbirds had stopped their usual morning choir, and stillness filled the air. His every instinct told him that something was wrong. Without disturbing Demasduit and the baby, he rose from the sleeping bench and left the mamateek.

What he saw filled him with dread. Seven armed white men, less than a thousand yards away, were rapidly converging on the encampment. Realizing that he had been spotted, he re-entered the mamateek, shook Demasduit awake and told her to get up and run. Then he shouted to warn the others. His roars reverberated in the early morning air, and curious heads popped out of the other mamateeks to see what was happening. Within seconds, the encampment was in chaos and confusion.

The Beothuk, including Nonosbawsut with his infant daughter in his arms, fled to the woods on the nearby shoreline, the invaders in close pursuit. Only Demasduit, still weak from having recently given birth, failed to reach the safety of the forest. Nonosbawsut watched in dismay as she fell to the ice, unable to run any farther. Before she could recover and move on, her pursuers reached her and pulled her to her feet. He saw her resist, and then, as she realized the futility of her situation, submit and passively permit herself to be led away. He watched her attempts to shake the hands of her captors, and her gestures as she tried to communicate with them. At one point she bared her breasts to indicate to them that she was the mother of a still suckling infant.

The sight of his wife being manhandled by the white men was more than Nonosbawsut could bear. He left the woods and approached her captors. He held the tip of a fir tree to his forehead, the traditional

Beothuk symbol of peace, but the white men, ignorant of its significance, ignored his offering. Like Demasduit, he shook their hands, and let them know with gestures that he wanted his wife back. At that point he was doing everything within his power to recover her without resorting to violence. He approached the man holding her and attempted to extract her from his grasp. He was prevented from doing so by three of the man's companions, who grabbed him and threw him off, knocking him to the ground.

Now angered, he arose and extracted a small axe from inside his cloak and, brandishing it over his head, ran to the nearest man and attempted to wrestle the man's gun from him. Again he was pulled off, and with several guns now trained on him, he had no choice but to relinquish his weapon. Then, as his rage consumed him, he darted and took another of his tormentors by the throat. With Nonosbawsut's iron grip on him, the man was sure of his intention to kill him unless his companions rescued him, which, with much difficulty, they were able to do. Failing to pull Nonosbawsut away as before, they resorted to battering him with the butts of their rifles. Even that did not work and he was deterred only when one of the white men sunk his bayonet deeply into Nonosbawsut's lower back, and drove him to his knees.

He still wasn't finished. By some monumental effort of will he ignored his injuries and got to his feet again and attempted to resume strangling the same man. Three shots were fired, and three bullets entered Nonosbawsut's body, sending him to the ground for the third time. This time he did not rise. His shattered body shuddered for several seconds and then went still. The last Beothuk chieftain was dead, his slate-grey eyes staring vacantly into the morning sky.

One of his slayers, awed by Nonosbawsut's size, insisted on measuring him. Taking a piece of line from his pocket, he tied a small knot in one end of it to denote the bottom of the slain warrior's feet, and another at the top of his head. Later, when he was able to take a more accurate measurement, he asserted that the distance between the two knots was six feet, seven and one-half inches.

The slaying of Nonosbawsut was the death knell for the Beothuk race. Within ten years they would be extinct. His twenty-three-year-old wife, Demasduit, lived less than a year in confinement before dying of tuberculosis. Her niece, Shanawdithit, who surrendered herself to the white settlers four years later, survived six years in their world before succumbing to the same disease. Much of what is now known about Beothuk culture, their customs, traditions, and beliefs, was passed along by these two young women during their brief captivities.

When Shanawdithit drew her final breath in June 1829, the Beothuk people were no more.

AUTHOR'S NOTE

This fiction narrative touches briefly on the 330-year history of the Beothuk, from their first encounter with the Corte-Reals in 1500 to the death of Shanawdithit in 1829. The Beothuk names used in the initial periods of this account are fictitious. It was not until the early nineteenth century that the names of a few of the Beothuk people then living became known, such as Demasduit, Shanawdithit, and Nonosbawsut, which are names familiar to most Newfoundlanders and Labradorians today.

Newfoundland historians differ in their opinions regarding the extent to which persecution by white settlers contributed to the eventual extinction of the Beothuk Indians. The compilation of accounts and stories contained in James P. Howley's *The Beothucks or Red Indians* (Cambridge: Cambridge University Press, 1915) seems to suggest that its impact was very significant, perhaps the greatest contributing factor of all. This view seems to be supported in some measure by Joseph R. Smallwood's *Encyclopedia of Newfoundland and Labrador* (St. John's: Newfoundland Book Publishers Limited, 1967, 1981) and his *Book of Newfoundland* (St. John's: Newfoundland Book Publishers Limited, 1967). Harold Horwood, in his article entitled "The People Who Were Murdered for Fun," published in *Maclean's* magazine (October 10, 1959) also asserts this to be the case. In his article, Horwood strongly contends that from the very beginning, seasonal European fishermen and white settlers routinely killed the Beothuk whenever an opportunity arose, and quite often it was done just for the sport of it. He further argues that during the late 1700s and early 1800s, when the stakes for ownership of lucrative water rights and prime fur locations became much higher, the random and opportunistic killing of the Beothuk became organized and systematic, carried out primarily by the furriers of Notre Dame Bay.

Some other historians take a different view. Frederick Rowe, in his *Extinction: The Beothuks of Newfoundland* (Toronto: McGraw-Hill Ryerson, 1977), makes the argument that the impact of the white settlers on the demise of the Beothuk has been greatly overstated and suggests that the reputation of the Notre Dame Bay people, indeed all Newfoundlanders, has been much maligned because of this. Rowe dismisses the more extreme accounts of the massacre of the Beothuk as myths.

Ingeborg Marshall's *A History and Ethnology of the Beothuk* (Montreal and Kingston: McGill-Queen's Press, 1996) recognizes the seriousness of the slaughter of the Beothuk by the white settlers but concludes that the primary cause of their extinction was disease, as well as the lengthy hostility which existed between the Beothuk and the Mi'kmaq Indians of Newfoundland whose hunting grounds and living areas often overlapped.

Information about John Peyton, Sr. and Jr., was taken primarily from *River Lords: Father and Son* by Amy Louise Peyton (St. John's: Jesperson Publishing, 1987).

THE NEW ROAD

"The mail boat seems to be running a bit late today, doesn't it?"

"Yes, Mother," Mary answered as she scanned the cove through the tiny pantry window and saw that, even in the shelter of the cove, tiny spumes of white foam whipped the water and wind squalls darted about randomly, darkening and agitating the surface wherever they touched. That was why he was late. She knew that if it was this brisk here in the cove, it must be much rougher outside in the arm.

"Perhaps he won't be coming today," she suggested.

"Oh, he'll be here, all right," Maude insisted. "It'll be a frosty Friday when he won't come. He's just held up a little, I dare say."

Even as her mother spoke, Mary spotted the unmistakable prow of Stephen Smith's white mail-boat bob past the point, skirt Devil's Rock, and begin to make its way across the cove.

"Yes, Mother, you're right. That's him coming in now."

"That's good. And Mary dear–"

"I know, I know, put the kettle on. I'll get to it right away."

Within minutes, Mr. Smith was depositing the heavy mailbag on the shining canvas floor of Maude Martin's kitchen, oblivious to the little pools forming at his feet as water dripped from his wet oilskins. Mary had often wondered why he always brought the bag to the kitchen, no matter what the weather was like, and left rain or snow or slush all over the place, instead of taking it directly to the post office door which was only twenty feet away. She had mentioned it to her mother only to be told, "It's because he wants to make sure he gets his little munch before he goes back," and that had brought the issue to a close and it was never mentioned again.

"You poor man," Maude fussed. "Now then, how about a nice cup of hot tea to warm you up?"

"Don't mind if I do, maid, haven't had a bite in me gut since early this morning." He hoped that the tea, when it came, would be laced with a good drop of brandy. Sometimes it was, but not always. Today he could use it.

Mary emerged from the pantry with a plate of gingersnaps and cream crackers, poured a cup of tea, and set it all on the table. Mr. Smith sipped the tea expectantly and found it to his liking.

"Was it very bad coming down the arm today, Mr. Smith?" she asked.

"Yes, me darlin'. 'Tis not fit for anything out there. Any man with a grain of sense would stay home on a day like this, and the worst of it is that I got to turn around and go right back up again."

"Well, you know that you can always bide here anytime you're stuck," said Maude. "We've got lots of room."

"Nah," he replied, pausing between sips. "It's not really that bad. I've been out in a lot worse. It's just that sometimes I think I'm getting a bit too old to be at this racket."

"Well, you won't have to worry about that very much longer, will you? The new road will be here soon."

"No, maid, I won't." He paused to study the bottom of his empty cup before continuing. Maude took the hint and told Mary to fill it up again.

After two or three drawn-out swallows to assure himself that the desired ingredient was still present, he continued. "Actually, next week will be my last run. After that the mail will be coming down by truck – and I'll be out of a job."

"What a pity. What are you going to do?" The concern in Maude's voice was genuine.

"Well…" He hesitated. "I suppose I don't have much choice. Me and Everett talked about setting out the old cod trap again, that is, if it's not rotted out by now. It's been ten years or more since it was in the water. If that doesn't work out, I don't know what I'll do. Go in over the line, I suppose, and look for some kind of work in the lumber woods."

"It's not fair," Maude sympathized. "You'd think they'd have made a better arrangement than that, a pension or something, wouldn't you? And at your age, too. It's just not right."

Then an odd thought crossed her mind. "'Tis funny how things work out sometimes when you really stop and think about them. They say that one man's loss is another man's gain. And, here's you, going to be put out of work by the new road, but for all of us down here in the cove it's probably going to be the best thing that's ever happened to us. After all these years of isolation, we'll finally be connected to the rest of the world."

Mary interrupted, "Mother, have you looked at the time?"

"Yes, dear," Maude sighed. "I'll get started."

Mary smiled to herself. She knew her mother well. She'd keep the people outside waiting a little longer. She always did. Then she'd fling open the door and, in her most officious voice, announce, "The post office is now open for business."

Mary's father, Jim, when he was alive, used to tease her mother and tell her she was vain, said she was "too proud for her own good." And Mary always knew, despite her mother's hot denials, there was an element of truth in what her father said. During the week, whenever her mother met people somewhere in the small community, it was always "Hello, Aunt Sue, how are you feeling today, my dear?" or "Good morning, Uncle Ted, and where are you off to this fine day?" But on Thursday, when the post mistress in her took over, it was "Letter for Mrs. Susannah Harvey" and "Parcel for Mr. Theodore Penney." Yes, Mary did know her mother's ways. But she knew something else, something far more important. She knew that her mother, despite the fact that she occasionally put on airs, was a good, decent woman with a kind heart who'd give anyone the clothes off her back if they needed them. And that, in the final analysis, Mary believed, counted above everything else.

Thursday was mail day – every week, weather permitting. As soon as the mail boat put in its appearance, people from all around the cove left whatever they were doing and converged slowly on the post office, which happened to be located in the front room of Maude Martin's house on the south side of the cove, once used as a bedroom but now renovated and fitted with its own exterior door. Anyone expecting a letter or package came with the hope that this would be the day it arrived. Others came on the off-chance that there might be something for them, too, while others, who probably hadn't received any mail in months, even years, simply came to see what was going on and to get whatever little bits of news or gossip happened to be going around the cove at that time. Some rowed over in their punts, while others came on foot. Nobody rushed. Rarely did anything different or exciting happen to break the monotony of the quiet life of the cove.

Mary always helped her mother with the distribution of the mail. She'd try to sort it as best she could and then hand each piece to Maude who would then call out the recipient's name. Maude did all the calling. Invariably, the major portion of the mailbag's contents, often more than half of it, would be for Simon Martin, the merchant. He rarely came with the rest of the crowd unless he was in a hurry to get something in particular. So his pile was usually put aside for him to collect later that evening or the following morning.

Mary enjoyed her work in the post office and looked forward to it every week. It wasn't so much the work itself as it was the opportunity to listen in on the various conversations that took place in the little crowded room. That was what she really liked, for Mary was a listener. As she sorted and passed the mail along to her mother, she could easily keep track of the many different discussions taking place. And today the main topic of discussion was the new road.

"They'll be bustin' through any day now," boomed Uncle Noah.

"Yes," agreed Aunt Em Harvey, whose house was the farthest one up on the flat and the closest one to the point where the new road would eventually enter the cove. "I can hear them bulldozers going all day long. They sound like they're getting closer and closer."

"Won't it be wonderful?" Mary picked up from another separate chat taking place between Miriam and her sister Jane. "Sure, we'll be able to nip up to Clarenville whenever we want and be back again inside a couple of hours. I dare say if we left early enough in the morning we could even dart into St. John's and be back home again before dark."

My God, there's never been a car in the cove, thought Mary, and already they're nipping up to Clarenville and darting in to St. John's. Oh well, it won't be long, I suppose.

Someone else said, "And not only that, they say that once the road is through, we'll get electricity, and telephones too before long. You just mark my words."

And so the snippets of conversation went, straying occasionally to other topics, but invariably coming back to the new road. Then, finally, when Uncle Mose Hiscock cleared his throat, an expectant hush fell over the small room. When Uncle Mose spoke, people listened. Just about everybody in the cove deferred to him whenever he delivered his opinions or made his pronouncements. It was another of those things that Mary didn't quite understand. Perhaps it was his voice, for everything he said was delivered in a deep, funereal voice that made even the simplest utterance sound like some deep philosophical statement of great importance. Or maybe it was the fact the he was the three-quarters minister, who delivered the sermons and conducted the weddings, funerals, and baptisms during the first three weeks of every month and kept things going until the real minister made his scheduled appearance the last Sunday of the month. Whatever the reason, Mary thought, she wasn't convinced of his invincibility, for she had noticed, even if nobody else in the cove had, that he wasn't always right. He was wrong sometimes, just like everyone else. Yet everybody seemed to accept everything he said as gospel.

"We'll have our road by next Wednesday." He offered no elaboration or rationale to support his statement, but just about everyone there took it for granted that next Wednesday the new road would indeed arrive. It also marked the end of the gathering, as shortly thereafter people began to drift away from the post office to return from whence they had come.

The days that followed were no different. The new road was the top thing on everybody's mind. Whenever people met, on the pathways or in the store or on the wharf, it was always the first thing to be mentioned. "How close are they now, do you think?" "Have you been up to see it yet?" "Howard says he's going in to St. John's the first chance to get a pickup truck."

And then the dream became a reality. They "busted through." To no one's surprise, except probably Mary's, it happened early Wednesday morning, just as Uncle Mose had prophesied. By ten o'clock, everyone in the cove was up there to observe the miracle in its final stages. Two large bulldozers pushed brush and trees aside as if they were matchsticks, piling whatever was in their paths in great heaps along both sides of the new road that they were forging out of the wilderness, while a fleet of six or seven dump trucks worked feverishly to keep up, dropping their loads of crushed stone and gravel, and then leaving, only to return minutes later with more of the same. And finally, an enormous yellow grader swept back and forth over the final section of road, spreading it all out and making it smooth and level.

It was done, but then, just as people were beginning to leave, a fanfare of horns and a great cloud of dust heralded the arrival of a large black car, the first ever to enter the cove. It was a delegation sent by the government to dedicate the completion of the new road with an "official opening." A man in a bowler hat and a dark grey suit and tie, using a bullhorn to introduce himself as the member for their district, separated himself from the others and immediately launched into a long speech, the gist of which, when you sifted through all the rhetoric and oratory, was that the people of the cove owed their new road and all the benefits that would ensue to none other than himself and his government. It was he and his party, he said, and they alone, who had brought the cove into the twentieth century, and suggested in no uncertain terms that in the upcoming election people should vote accordingly. After he was finished, he and the other men from the delegation mingled with the crowd, shook hands with the people, clapped a few backs, and distributed candy to the children. Then, with more honking of its horn, the car and its entourage turned around and sped back up the arm in another cloud of dust as quickly as it had come.

That night, as they knitted and sewed in the comfortable warmth of the kitchen, Mary and her mother recounted the events of the day. "Wonderful," Maude murmured absently as she tried to pick up a few stitches she had dropped in the dim lamplight. Mary wasn't quite so sure the new road would be all that beneficial to her and her mother. The chances of them getting a car with their financial means, she thought, and with no one to drive it in any case, were slim. They'd undoubtedly have to fork over good money to someone every time they needed passage somewhere, no doubt about it. Still, she admitted, that was certainly a lot better than having to take a boat everywhere they wanted to go.

Maude and Mary were still discussing the new road as they washed up after breakfast early the following morning when Aunt Sue, their nearest neighbour, tapped on their door, popped her head through, and breathlessly asked, "Have you heard the news? There's been an accident."

"An accident?" Maude dropped her dishcloth into the sink. "What kind of accident?" she asked in a small frightened voice. "Did someone drown?"

"Well, it's Hayward Penny and Eli Martin. They were in a car accident up on the new road last night. They're dead – both of them."

It took some seconds for Aunt Sue's words to register. Maude plopped down into the rocking chair, clasped her big arms around her bosom, and rocked back and forth as she tried to fathom what she had just been told. Mary fled from the kitchen into her bedroom where she threw herself on the bed and buried her head in the big feather pillow, fending off the awful news.

Word of the accident spread rapidly through the cove. Little knots of people appeared everywhere. People went to the store to buy things they didn't really need just to make contact with each other. Fishermen lingered at each other's stageheads, delaying going out to their nets as long as possible. School was suspended. The normal work of the cove came to a standstill. The cove was in mourning. And in shock.

The two days leading up to the funeral were difficult. Mary, like many others in the cove, was having a hard time coming to grips with the deaths of Hayward and Eli. Even though she had never had a particularly close relationship with either of the two young men, her grief for them was genuine. They had been her school chums and playmates.

Death was not new to her. Only the past winter, just a few short months before, Eileen Baker's eighteen-month-old daughter, who Mary sometimes looked after, had succumbed to the diphtheria epidemic that had swept through most of Trinity Bay. And not long before that, her Aunt Ellen, who she liked a lot, had passed away in her sleep. Indeed, when she was twelve, Mary had lost her own father when his schooner sank with all hands on board while shipping a load of fish to St. John's. Somehow these deaths had seemed normal, even her father's, although she still missed him a lot. She, like other people in the hundreds of small isolated communities that dot Newfoundland's coastline, reliant on the sea for their existence, accepted the inevitability of drownings and premature death by accident or disease. She knew it was only a fortunate minority who managed to live out their full four-score-and-ten to die of a ripe old age in their own beds. It was the natural order of things. People mourned the passing of their loved ones, comforted each other, accepted the inevitable, remembered them, and got on with their own lives.

To Mary and others, the deaths of Hayward and Eli were different. This tragedy was not a normal occurrence. It was as if two young lives had been wasted.

And then, as the hours passed, the questions arose, and the stories and rumours started to circulate. Where did they get the car? Who owned it? Did they steal it? How did they know how to drive when they'd probably been in a car only a few times in their entire lives? Who was driving? Nobody knew for certain because both bodies had been found some distance from the vehicle. Harry Penney had gone up to see the wreckage and told everyone, "They must have been flying, the car was that far from the road. It must have turned over a dozen times. It was bent and twisted so bad you couldn't even tell what kind of car it was." They found out afterward that it was a Chev, because a few days later Harry, when he went up again, found the Chevrolet insignia plate on the ground. It had been flung loose by the impact of the crash. He hung it over his stagehead door where it stayed for years until it eventually rusted out and fell off.

Someone brought up the notion that they might have been drinking. Shortly after that, somebody else said that someone they knew saw two young men that could have been Hayward and Eli coming out of the tavern in Goobies that evening, barely able to stand up. So it was soon accepted by more than a few that liquor was indeed at the heart of the accident. Most of the questions, however, were never definitively answered. Most people in the cove eventually came to their own conclusions and somehow managed to put the matter to rest in their own minds.

This time, the real minister, given the nature of the tragedy, came down to conduct the funeral service even though it wasn't the end of the month. People squeezed into the pews, filling them to their utmost capacity. Those who arrived a bit late had to stand back in the vestibule or outside in the churchyard. The bells pealed mournfully while they all waited for the burial service to begin. The bodies, in plain unopened coffins, had been carried in and placed at the front of the church before the crowd arrived. Miriam Harvey, who had laid the corpses out, said it was a good thing they weren't shown: "The poor things were smashed up so bad you couldn't even recognize them." A rumour circulated for a while that Eli had been decapitated, but Miriam, one of the few people who had actually seen the bodies, said that was not the case.

For Mary, the service in the church was surreal. Even as she plodded along with the rest of the congregation from the church to the cemetery where the final prayers, hymns, and interment would take place, she was strangely detached from it all, as if watching it from a great distance, feeling the emotional undercurrents of the crowd – absorbing the whole thing to the extent that she would remember it in minute detail for the rest of her life.

Finally it was over, and Mary was shaken back to reality by her mother tugging at her sleeve. "Come on, my dear, let's go home." They walked together in silence, each preoccupied by the events of the past few days, still trying to make some sense of it all. Life would go on, of course, but somehow the cove would never be the same again. In some indefinable way it had been damaged beyond repair.

"Hello, Maude and Mary." The tiny voice of a frail old woman broke their reverie.

"My God, Aunt Ida. I didn't even notice you," Maude exclaimed. "And you've been so sick. How are you feeling now, my dear?"

"Much better. I guess it was just old age catching up with me," the old woman offered. "This whole business is some sad, isn't it? Two strapping young men gone, just like that."

"Yes, maid, it's unbelievable. It makes you wonder, doesn't it? And to think of their poor parents. I wouldn't want to be in their shoes," Maude replied.

"Nor me. They'll never get over it. Oh well, there's Harve waiting for me, so I best get along now. I'll see you in church next Sunday."

"Yes, Aunt Ida," Maude said. "I'll be there." Then, as an afterthought, she added, "I saw you up at the official opening the other day but I never got a chance to speak with you. What do you think of it all?"

"The new road? My dear, 'tis wonderful. A real blessing. Sure, it's opened up a whole new world for us, hasn't it. Things will never be the same again, will they?"

No, thought Mary, the image of Hayward and Eli being lowered into the ground still vivid in her mind. They certainly won't.

AUTHOR'S NOTE

During the 1950s and 1960s, the construction of new roads and highways linked previously isolated or semi-isolated communities to each other and to larger urban growth centres. This, along with the introduction of electricity, telephone, and other services, had a profound impact on small settlements all over Newfoundland. These advances greatly improved the lives of the residents in many ways, particularly with respect to accessing goods and services, using modern conveniences, communications, and mobility, and provided a new-found opportunity to be part of the larger world outside.

Still, as is often the case during periods of rapid progress, some things were lost – intangible perhaps, but, nevertheless, important and significant in terms of the culture of a people who had long survived self-sufficiently. The spirit of communal unity and sharing that had sustained these small communities over hundreds of years began to erode as their residents shifted into a new and more modern lifestyle. This is the setting for the fictional story "The New Road," a story loosely based on an event that occurred in my home community in the mid-1950s.

WHAT HAPPENED
AT DEVIL'S COVE?

*L*abour Day, 1990. The afternoon sun sparkled on the blue waters of Devil's Cove and the warm southerly breeze blowing in off the water gently swept in through the open car window. Now that she was alone, Laura could hear the gentle waves as they lapped softly against the rocky beach below, creating soothing murmurs that instilled within her a deep sense of peace and solitude as she waited for her husband, John, and her grandson, Daniel. They had left a few minutes earlier to go beachcombing in Skiff Cove, a slightly larger inlet on the other side of the small ridge separating it from Devil's Cove. That was where they often gathered beach rocks, shells, bird feathers, and other such interesting things. A few gulls, no longer as plentiful as they had been when there were fishing stages around, screeched somewhere overhead, their discordant shrieking somehow complementing the harmony of the moment.

Laura lazily watched her husband and Daniel reach the crest of the knoll and disappear as they began their descent down to the more rugged Skiff Cove beach. She was a little bit worried about Daniel because she knew the pathway down was very steep and strewn with loose rubble. Trying to banish such worrisome thoughts, she pushed the car seat back as far as it would go and adjusted its incline as low as possible. She was determined that a rare moment like this should not be wasted. Reckoning that they would be gone at least half an hour, Laura intended to take full advantage of the opportunity for a few well-earned minutes of relaxation. She decided that she wouldn't even open the latest bestseller she'd brought along with her.

Lulled to sleep by the lapping waters of Devil's Cove, she was awakened by a dog barking nearby, and then she heard voices. Sleepily, she looked and saw a woman and two young children, a boy and a girl about five or six years old, more than likely twins, wending their way through the tall grassy expanse which everyone always called Ned's Meadow, although nobody seemed to know who Ned had actually been.

The little girl sang as she picked buttercups and dandelions, while the boy quickly ran past the car and down to the beach where he proceeded to skim flat stones out into the water. She could hear him counting the number of skips with each throw, yelling jubilantly whenever he achieved an exceptionally high number. The woman – whom Laura assumed was their mother – sat on a large rock a short distance from the car and let them play, seemingly content to keep a close eye on her children as they enjoyed themselves. Their dog, a little black curly-haired "crackie," meandered all over the meadow, frequently returning to receive a pat on the head from the woman. She acknowledged Laura's presence with a small wave of her hand and a simple hello before they moved off.

Laura was struck by their clothing. The woman wore a long dress, the bottom of which settled into the long grass where she stood, and the apron covering it was almost as long as the dress itself. Her bonnet resembled those that Laura had seen only in old pictures. Her daughter, whose long golden curls hung down her back, was similarly attired, but without the apron. The boy was wearing breeches held up by braces. She could see, even from the distance separating them, that the leather patches on the knees had received considerable punishment from an obviously active and adventuresome youth.

She heard the mother tell them, "Children, the other beach is much nicer. Let's go over there."

Gradually they made their way toward Skiff Cove, pausing frequently to pick flowers or to examine some object. They appeared to be in no rush to get there. They seemed to be a very happy little family. But who were they? Laura hadn't seen them around the area before. Maybe they were just visitors or tourists. Maybe Mennonites or members of a similar sect. Or were they just having fun wearing some old clothes they had found in their attic? Eventually they disappeared over the top of the knoll.

Laura settled back for a few more minutes of relaxation, but was no longer in the mood. She picked up her book and read until her husband and Daniel returned, bearing with them Daniel's treasures from the beach.

"Did you see that woman and her two children in Skiff Cove?" she asked them. They both looked at her blankly and denied seeing anybody else while they were there.

"But you must have." She stopped short. Had she been dreaming? Maybe her husband and Daniel simply missed them somehow.

"Let's drop in and see Aunt Cecelia on our way back," Daniel said, knowing he'd be treated to cookies and a glass of something sweet and have a chance to tease Aunt Cecelia's cat, Ginger.

Laura and John readily agreed. Aunt Cecelia was one of Laura's favourite relatives, and John knew he'd get one of the cold beers she always kept for him in the outer cool room.

When they entered Aunt Cecelia's kitchen a few minutes later the pleasant aroma of freshly baked bread permeated the house. The kitchen stove was going full blast despite the warm temperature outside, and Aunt Cecelia was bustling about as usual, making repeated trips to and from the pantry, continually wiping her hands in her apron, and fussing over them like they were her long-lost children. Everything was normal – except one thing.

Sitting at the table, slowly sipping a cup of tea was an elderly man Laura had never seen before. Ancient, she thought to herself, was perhaps a better description of him – very old indeed.

"This is Mr. Ryan," Aunt Cecelia said, offering no further elaboration other than, "He's here from Clarenville for a little visit."

The old man glanced up and acknowledged them with a slight nod, and then returned his concentration to the teacup which trembled in his hand. A buttered bun lay untouched on his plate. He was now to all appearances oblivious to their presence. There was an aura of sadness about him, a despondency so deep that Laura could almost feel it herself. She didn't know what was at the root of it, but her heart immediately went out to him.

Aunt Cecelia had scarcely resumed her fussing when they heard a knock on the door.

"That will be Mr. Ryan's nephew here to pick him up," she said. "He's staying at the B&B just up the road. Going back to Clarenville tomorrow." A few minutes later the old man was led gingerly by a much younger man to the car waiting outside.

"Aunt Cecelia," Laura asked, "is Mr. Ryan a relative of yours?"

"No," her aunt replied. "In fact, I can't say that I really know him very well at all because he doesn't say much when he's here. I'm not sure where he came from originally, perhaps Ireland, because he has a bit of that brogue. He lives in Clarenville now and comes down here every year around Labour Day. Stays overnight, has a cup of tea with me, and goes away again. He's been coming back to the village for years, nigh unto sixty I'd say, for as long as I can remember. Must be in his nineties now, perhaps more, and he's so frail he can hardly sit up in a chair. I don't know how he manages to get around at all, poor old fellow."

"But why? Why does he come here, if he's no relation to you?" Laura asked.

"Well, there's a story, but I'm not sure how much stock I would put in it," she began. "They say he came here many years ago, before 1930, with his wife and built a little house on that grassy stretch between this house and Devil's Cove, apart from everyone else. As far as everybody could tell, they were very happy and seemed to love each other very much. He was a fisherman, and while he was away at sea she passed the time by making a little vegetable garden. But she was homesick and missed her native Scotland, or so the story goes, and often mentioned that she would like to see her birthplace and her family again someday. Her husband always promised her that she would."

With a sigh, Aunt Cecelia continued, "They say that shortly after settling there she took to spending long hours standing on the high rise that separates Devil's Cove and Skiff Cove, just gazing out on the sea. People began to refer to her as the Lady on the Hill. Then the children were born, twins, I think. The three of them spent endless hours there or down on the beach.

"Then one day the husband was called to St. John's to settle a matter relating to his property. When he returned he found his house empty and cold, his wife and his children no longer there. There was no note and she didn't appear to have taken anything with her. He talked to the people of the village but no one knew anything.

"He was heartbroken. Days became weeks, and weeks months, until he finally had to accept that his wife and children were indeed gone. Finally, one day he just left without even boarding up the windows of his house, and never returned – until many years later."

Aunt Cecelia shrugged, then continued, "Some believed that the woman and her two children had been drowned off Devil's Cove by a rogue wave that swept them out to sea. Still, no bodies were ever found, not even the dog. Others suggested they were taken by raiders. Still others said the fairies had gotten them. Who knows what really happened?"

She put a hand to her chin. "What did the poor man think of it all, I wonder? I do remember my own father telling me that Mr. Ryan believed that his wife's homesickness for her Scottish birthplace had finally become so overwhelming that, while he was away in St. John's, she had found someone to take her and the children to Scotland – this despite her obvious love for her husband. Most people in the village were of the opinion that that was most likely the case.

"You know, he never gave up on them. He never stopped searching. He's had a tormented existence ever since. He sold everything off and saved every penny to take a trip to Scotland, but her relatives there could offer no information about her disappearance. I believe years ago he even went to Ireland and England searching for them. He still comes back here every year though. He used to go out to Devil's Cove and stand on the rise just like she used to, staying there by himself for hours. But he's too old to do that now. I guess he'll die without ever knowing what became of them. It's a really sad story, isn't it."

A cold shiver ran down Laura's spine. She felt a strange sense of loss. The old man's, she supposed. Was it because today was likely to be the last time he would ever visit here again?

Then, somehow, she knew that the woman had not willingly left him. Laura simply could not reconcile the happiness she'd witnessed on the beach with the idea of the woman deserting her husband. Had the woman somehow chosen her to ease the old man's suffering and bring him some comfort?

The kitchen was silent.

"There's a Blue Jays game on TV tonight, Pop," Daniel offered. "Can we make a pizza and watch it?"

"Sure," John said. "Who are they playing?"

"The Red Sox. It'll be a good game."

John stood up. "We should be getting on home then."

"Just a minute," said Laura. "We have a little stop to make first. Aunt Cecelia, where did you say Mr. Ryan is staying?"

AUTHOR'S NOTE

Throughout Newfoundland there are countless places shrouded in mystery – bogs and marshes, small hills, wooded copses, coves and the like – where eerie sightings have been made, unexplained lights seen, and strange noises heard. The stories about these presumably haunted spots are as varied as they are numerous. In this fictional story, the adjoining beaches of Devil's Cove and Skiff Cove near Port Rexton, Trinity Bay, fit this description. Despite the fact that this area of Trinity Bay has been inhabited and populated for hundreds of years, the grassy headland overlooking these two coves remains virtually untouched and bears no man-made structures of any kind, perhaps attesting to the aura of the place.

acknowledgements

For her encouragement, support, editing, and contribution of ideas during the writing of these short stories, I wish to thank my wife Joan, as well as my daughter Susan for her proof-reading and advice.

Thank you as well to the management and staff of Breakwater Books, especially Rebecca Rose, Annamarie Beckel, and Rhonda Molloy, for their efforts and expertise in bringing this book to publication.

In the mid to late 1700s, a group of desperate men, mostly deserters and escaped prisoners, as well as indentured men and boys who had run away from their fishing masters, secluded themselves in the wilderness on the southern shore of Newfoundland's Avalon Peninsula. Led by Peter Kerrivan, himself a deserter from the British Navy, these renegades, predominantly Irish, established their hideout on or near Butterpot, a small mountain about nine miles inland from Ferryland. Defying the law and evading all attempts made to capture them, they survived on the great caribou herds that roamed the barrens and by raiding the fishing settlements along the coast. Known as the Society of Masterless Men, their legend is one of the most exciting and daring in Newfoundland's rich and colourful past.